KARMA
IS A MOTHA

KARMA
IS A MOTHA

JOANNA MCLAURIN

Karma is a Motha

Copyright © 2020 by Joanna Mclaurin. All rights reserved.

No part of this publication may be reproduced, stored in a retrieval system or transmitted in any way by any means, electronic, mechanical, photocopy, recording or otherwise without the prior permission of the author except as provided by USA copyright law.

This novel is a work of fiction. Names, descriptions, entities, and incidents included in the story are products of the author's imagination. Any resemblance to actual persons, events, and entities is entirely coincidental.

The opinions expressed by the author are not necessarily those of URLink Print and Media.

1603 Capitol Ave., Suite 310 Cheyenne, Wyoming USA 82001
1-888-980-6523 | admin@urlinkpublishing.com

URLink Print and Media is committed to excellence in the publishing industry.

Book design copyright © 2020 by URLink Print and Media. All rights reserved.

Published in the United States of America
ISBN 978-1-64753-392-2 (Paperback)
ISBN 978-1-64753-391-5 (Digital)
29.05.20

CONTENTS

Introduction		7
Chapter 1:	A wife and a mistress	9
Chapter 2:	Money, men and making love	22
Chapter 3:	The not so perfect Shantale	32
Chapter 4:	Welcome to Hell	49
Chapter 5:	Plotting and Praying	56
Chapter 6:	15 years earlier	59
Chapter 7:	A crush	70
Chapter 8:	Falling for you	85
Chapter 9:	Graduation blues	96
Chapter 10:	I need love	111
Chapter 11:	A reality check	115
Chapter 12:	The summer after	128
Chapter 13:	College Days	144
Chapter 14:	Reunited	169
Chapter 15:	The second chance	180
Chapter 16:	Still in love	191
Chapter 17:	Karma is a Motha	205
Chapter 18:	Love in all the wrong places	219
Chapter 19:	Gena's special day	225

INTRODUCTION

Whitley, Gena, and Shantale were three beautiful and sassy women all from prominent backgrounds. They have had and lived the best that life could offer. However, all at once their perfect lives will somehow be destroyed. For three years in a row, one by one each lady will disappear on the same exact date. Someone is out to get revenge, someone they have scarred from their once devious past. Will these women make it out alive? Read and see!

CHAPTER 1

A wife and a mistress

Whitley Mowry stood in the mirror of her bathroom staring at the hideous hickey that laid on the left side of her neck.

Her boss had placed it there the night before.

Sure, the sex was incredible, and he often slid money into her personal Bank account, but they were both married.

Whitley married Kyle right after college. By 30 years old they were both at the peak of their careers and proud parents of two beautiful kids. Whitley stood proudly at 125 pounds, her skin was the same complexion as actress Halle Berry. She had this beautiful long brown hair and she had her father's hazel eyes.

Kyle on the other hand was the ideal black man. He was tall, dark, and handsome.

He was a business man at a fortune 500 company, and he always made sure his family had not a want in the world.

The two met in college and soon after they had fallen in love and decided it was only right to tie the knot. To most of their close relatives and friends,

they had the perfect union.

Kyle entered the bathroom and kissed his wife on her cheek. Whitley, always on guard pulled the hair over her neck to hide the hickey on her neck.

"How did that meeting go last night love?" Kyle quizzed his wife.

Whitley tried her best not to think back to what actually happened just hours before. Her mind reminisced on the night. Her boss had her on his desk and on the copy machine. They went at it hard every time they had sex.

"Oh, it was fine... we went over the charts and stuff like that no big deal." Whitley lied.

"Sounds good, they love you there, what would they do without you?"

Whitley tried not to blush. What would her boss do if he didn't have her hollering and screaming every few nights a week?

Kyle brushed his teeth then he left out of the bathroom.

Whitley stepped into the shower and turned it on warm.

As soon as the water hit her body, she went into a trance. It was almost as if she was experiencing some more of Dilland's good loving.

Dilland Mathis was her boss' name. He was this handsome white man that had the total package: from the looks, to the money, even what he packed in the slacks was worth complementing.

Their affair started a little over a year ago. The two of them were at the office late one night working on a project. Dilland kept complimenting her on her nice figure, and one thing led to another. 27 minutes later she laid on the floor naked and grasping for air. He had rocked her world and they became lovers ever since.

Once she was dressed to kill and her makeup was flawless,

Whitley went downstairs to join her family in the kitchen.

Kyle was pouring himself a cup of hot coffee when she entered the room. Kylie the oldest and their only daughter and Kyle Jr were fighting over a box of cereal.

Whitley snatched the box from them before they knew it.

"What is the problem down here?! You two act like cats and dogs. It doesn't make any sense to be fight over one box of cereal!" Whitley shouted at her kids.

"But I had them first" Kylie complained.

"No, I had them first liar!" Kyle Jr yelled back.

"OK, OK that is enough! I will pour the cereal myself, give me the bowls." Whitley said to end the argument.

Then she turned around to her husband.

"Kyle why didn't you handle this? And how long were they yelling over a box of cereal?" she

Interrogated him.

"They're kids… that's what they do" Kyle said before taking another sip of his coffee.

"Well I don't care what kids do, my two will not be brought up like wild animals.

I don't want them fighting with each other like that."

She rolled her eyes and grabbed her briefcase then headed off to work.

She kissed the kids then her husband before leaving the house.

As she got into the car, the cell phone started to ring.

A smile appeared on her face once she saw that it was Dillard calling.

"Hello "she answered as she pulled out of the driveway.

"Hello beautiful, what are you up to?" he asked in his sexy deep voice.

"Actually, I am on my way there" she replied.

"Hmm"

"I see you can't stop thinking about me." she teased him.

"I like to remind you that it was my name you kept yelling repeatedly last night."

Whitley couldn't help but laugh out loud.

"That may be the case, but you were moaning out my name as well."

"OK that's fair to say. I know you're driving and need to focus on that.

I will see you when you arrive here then."

"Sure, you will"

The day went smoothly at work for her. Once she arrived at the house Kyle had a scrumptious meal cooking. She came downstairs to join him once the food was ready.

"How was your day love?" he asked her.

"Smooth and easy, I wish everyday was like this one. But where are my kids?"

"They are washing up for dinner" Kyle told her.

"OK, well what are you making, it smells so good?"

"It's that beef stir fry and egg rolls that you like so much."

"Hmm I am gonna need seconds, I love that stuff."

"I know that's why I made it."

The kids ran in and joined their mother at the dinner table.

"When were you guys gonna speak to me?" Whitley asked her kids.

"Oh, hey Mommy, how are you?" Kylie said.

She was gorgeous with the most beautiful long curly hair. She always wore it in two long pigtails unless Whitley took her to the hair salon to get designer cornrows. She had a smooth caramel color. Kyle Jr was a little darker than his mother and he had her eyes. They looked alike the most while Kylie took more after her father.

"How was school?" Whitley asked them next.

"Well I had to stay inside during recess because my teacher had to give me a breathing treatment. I had a bad cough during nap time." Jr informed his mother.

"Aww, Kyle what was that all about?" she asked her husband.

"He had a little cough during nap time, so to be on the safe side his teacher gave him some medicine and made him stay in during playtime. It was cold out. But he did good throughout the rest of the day." Kyle told her.

"Next time this happens call me. I need to know when things like this happens to my kids."

"Food is ready, let's eat up."

Kyle brought over the food and they all started to dig in.

After the plates were empty the kids ran upstairs to prepare for the night.

Kyle started the dishes right away.

Whitley was still uneasy about the whole school ordeal. And she knew this would be a great time to talk to her husband about it.

She walked over and stood against the sink with her arms folded.

"When Jr had his treatment, why didn't you call me and let me know what was going on?" she asked him.

"Because it was no big deal. I didn't think you

would care since it was only for precaution."

"Kyle, that is my baby. I would like to know when things like this happens to our kids. How would you feel if something happened to Kylie and I didn't call and let you know what was going on? You would feel neglected right? That's how I feel right now about Jr. Why would you even feel like I didn't need to know that?"

"I didn't want you to worry (pauses) besides, I do most of the parenting anyways, I didn't think you would care."

"You do most of the what? Excuse me? It's the least you could do since I carried them both for 9 long months, gained excess weight, got stretch marks, and had to endure excruciating pain just so they could be here. But don't make it out like I'm not a good mom to them. I work a lot, but I am still their mother."

"And I never said you didn't do what you do for them. Since we are naming what we do for them; I take them to and from school every day. When they have a doctor's appointment or a after school meeting I'm the one there,

I feed them, I clothe them, I put them to bed every night, then I go work 10 plus hours a day so I can provide for them and you... so don't make it out like it's a competition. These are our kids we shouldn't have a limit or a list of the things that we do for them. And if you are done whining I gotta go get *our* kids ready for school."

He put the towel into the sink and then went upstairs.

Whitley knew there was nothing she could say after that.

So to ease her mine she decided to finish cleaning the kitchen and then head to bed.

As much as Whitley loved her affair with Dilland, it was slowly coming to an end. As the week progressed, there hadn't been any late night meetings, any calls to meet him at their favorite hotel or anything.

After contemplating on the issue over the weekend, Whitley made up her mind to confront Dilland face to face. She had to know why he was neglecting her all of a sudden. So Monday morning before clocking in, she walked down the hall to the last office on the left.

Francis, his assistant sat at her desk on the telephone when Whitley approached her.

"Hello Whitley, how may I assist you this morning?" Francis asked.

"Hi, is Mr. Mathis available right now?" she asked in the sweetest voice.

"Hold on let me go check."

She got up and walked into his office.

Whitley looked around the office at the pictures and paintings while Francis had a word with her boss. A few seconds passed before she came out.

"He is actually waiting on you, go on in."

"Thank you, Fran."

"No problem"

Whitley sighed before entering the office.

Dilland sat at his desk rocking back and forth in his chair.

"Mrs. Mowry how can I help you this afternoon?"

"Mrs. Mowry? That's new, what's going on with you?" Whitley asked as if he was speaking another language to her.

"That is the name on your paycheck and the deposit slips I transfer you all that money to right?" he quizzed her.

"OK, what's the hell is up Dilland? First, I don't hear from you or see you for a whole week then you call me Mrs. Mowry. Did I miss something?

"My wife is getting suspicious and she has been asking about my late night where abouts. You do know the saying it's cheaper to keep her right? Well I can not afford to lose half of my business and affairs to her.

The ride was one hell of one, but this is where I end it."

"What? I thought we were building something here?"

"Whitley you are a great asset to this company,

but the fling we had is over. I know this must be hard for you so I'm gonna let you take the rest of the day off. I will see you tomorrow have a good day."

At that moment, Whitley felt like a rug had been pulled from underneath her.

Why did he feel the need to end their perfect affair when it was just beginning?

Before she thought of something cruel to say, she decided to just leave and get far away from the office as she could.

Once she arrived at the house, she fixed herself a stiff drink and drank the entire glass in a few gulps. After 2 more she felt pretty good.

As she headed upstairs the doorbell rang. She saw that it was only the mailman with the mail. Whitley flipped through the letters.

Inside the pile was the usual coupons, insurance bills, but there was this yellow envelope that grabbed her attention. Whitley opened it and saw that it was a D.V.D. that read "play me" so she took it over to the TV and placed it into the D.V.D. player.

Moments later this movie started to play. A woman was on top of this man and she was riding him like he was a horse. As the movie continued to play she realized this was no random adult film, but of her making love to Dilland. Whitely hurried and jerked the D.V.D out of the player and broke it into pieces.

"That sick Bastard breaks up with me then sends this shit to my house?!

Go to hell you stupid asshole!" she yelled.

By six Kyle was home with the kids. They brought home burgers for dinner.

"You got home early today." Kyle said kissing her on the cheek.

"Yeah, I had a bad day at work, so I took the rest of the day off."

"What's wrong with you?" he asked.

"I had a bad headache, but I drank some wine, so I feel better now."

"I hope you are OK with Burger Queen the kids wanted to eat there tonight" Kyle said to her.

"That's fine I haven't had any junk food in a while so it shouldn't hurt."

"Yeah I got you a max burger and the chili fries along with a delicious strawberry milkshake."

"Oh, that sounds SOOO good."

"Hey Kylie and Jr, sit down and say your grace."

Dinner was nice, while they ate their meal Whitley did some thinking. She was really blessed to have such a beautiful family. She didn't need a man on the side. Kyle had proven to her over and over again that he was all the man she needed. She realized at that moment that she had more than enough right here. So what there wouldn't be extra shopping money in her private bank account.

She had a great husband and perfect kids. She would no longer take them for granted.

After dinner she decided that they should have a family night out. They took the kids to the movies and then out for ice cream afterwards.

She put her arm into Kyle's as they walked to the car after eating their dessert.

"I am so happy that we did this." she said to her husband.

"Me too, who are you and what have you done with my wife?" he teased her.

"That was a good one, but no, the other night I did some real soul searching.

I have the perfect husband, and kids, and I really have been taking you guys for granted, and I am so sorry. When I get home every night,

all I do is eat and go to bed. I don't help the kids with their homework.

I don't cook for you; I don't make love to you like I should.

And I promise to you that won't happen ever again."

"I like the new you and yeah we can work something out tonight.

"Oh well give me my punishment judge."

When things seemed to be coming together for Whitley, she got a huge surprise.

Sunday came and she sent Kyle and the kids out for brunch. This was their tradition so that she could stay home and clean the house from top to bottom.

As she mopped the kitchen floor her cell rang.

"Hello?"

"I have a room at the Hamptons. I left you a key at the front desk. Don t ask any questions, just get here" Dilland told her.

"OK, I will be there shortly" she smiled.

Whitley ran up the stairs and got in the shower. She was so happy. She knew he couldn't live without having her good loving for too long. After she looked like a Hollywood A- list actress, she left for the hotel.

Dilland opened the door right as Whitley approached it. She quickly wrapped her arms around him and started kissing him passionately all over. He closed the door and then headed towards the bed.

"Baby, I knew you couldn't resist me for too much longer.

Do you know how much I've missed you?"

Then out of nowhere he slapped her to the floor.

Whitley grabbed her face and watched as blood slid down from the corner of her mouth. What was wrong? Why had he hit her?

"I knew you were pathetic, but you must be a freaking idiot if you think I'm gonna let you destroy my marriage. How dare you send a sex tape of us to my house?! What if my wife actually got the mail first huh?! You were just a piece of ass to me. I would never leave my wife for you. Is that what you thought? Well if so you had it backwards. I want your office cleaned out by tomorrow morning. And if you come near me or my family again you're gonna wish I ended your life tonight." he snapped.

"I didn't send that to you! Someone sent that same tape to me!

I thought you sent it. I would never put you or your family in danger, I swear!" she said in her defense.

Dilland couldn't care less about what she had to say at this point. She was trying to destroy him and nothing was more despicable in his eyes.

He left out of the room and slammed the door behind.

After getting cleaned up, Whitley grabbed her bag and left the hotel as well. She cried the entire drive home. She had lost her lover and job all in one week. How could she tell Kyle that she lost her job? Little did she know but her day was far from over.

Whitley closed the car door and entered the house from the garage. There was no sign of the kids, so she went up to the master's bedroom.

To her surprise Kyle was there packing. He hadn't told her anything about a business trip.

"Where are you going?" she simply asked.

He looked at her and kept packing.

Kyle noticed the bruise on her lip where she was hit.

"What happened to your face?" he finally asked her.

"I slipped and fell while mopping the floor earlier." She lied.

"I bet"

"What does that mean?"

"You may think I'm some dumb, helpless dude, but I'm not. You are a sorry excuse for a woman, wife, and mother. I thought maybe you just didn't know how to be a wife or a mother to our kids. But truth be told you can't do it because you are too got damned selfish and busy being in your own spotlight. If Whitley is happy screw everyone else. That has been your motto since I met you. And because I was so in love with you, I didn't pay that much attention to it. But when you go behind my back and do the shit you did, that's where I draw the line. I know all about your little affair.

And I must admit you have some killer moves, none that I ever saw." Kyle expressed.

She didn't even try to deny it, he knew the truth now, all she could do was try to explain her side of the story.

"Baby, please let me explain this to you." she said grabbing his arm.

"Get the hell off of me!" He snatched away from her and walked to the other side of the bed.

"Y'all black women kill me. All I ever hear y'all say is how you need a good black man that don't cheat, got a good job, no baby mama drama, and you got that. But you still feel the need to dog me out. I'm done with this shit, go to hell Whitley."

"It was a mistake! I didn't mean for it to get that far out of hand. Kyle please don't do this to me! You and the kids are all that I have."

"That's bullshit! You didn't think about us while you were riding Uncle Tom now did you? You should be a porn star because you were incredible. How do you think in that small head of yours that I would just forgive you and accept that weak ass apology after what you did to me? I'm leaving, you can have the house. I am taking the kids, they probably won't even notice you're not there."

"Kyle don't do this, please let's try to work this out! What about our kids? They need to have both of their parents."

"We weren't on yo damn mind then so don't think about us now."

He put the bags on his shoulders and walked out to his car.

Whitley ran after him in tears. She wasn't about to lose her family without a fight.

"Kyle, please don't do this to me" she screamed as she pulled on the back of his shirt.

"Get your ass back in the house!" he yelled back to her.

"But I need you! I'm sorry, I love you not him" she continued to cry.

"You should have thought about all of this when you were doing your dirt!

I'll let the kids call you in a couple of days" Kyle said before hopping into his car.

"I need them, if your gonna go fine, but please don't take my kids too!" she screamed.

"You don't know how to be a mama for them either."

He closed the car door, turned on the ignition and backed out of the driveway.

    That night Whitley stayed up the entire night just crying. The thought of being without Kyle and her kids was an nightmare. She loved him and she loved the life they had built together. She drank a whole bottle of brown liquor while sitting in the bed. The last time she had been this depressed was when her parents told her they were divorcing on her high school graduation day.

The next day Whitley put on some sweatpants and an old t shirt then she went to the office to get her things.

Her coworkers all stared at her as if they knew the reason why she was leaving. But she couldn't care less. She would never have to see them again. Her office looked dark and cold when she opened the door.

She walked over to her desk and pulled open the drawers. All she had inside were some breath mints, an extra pair of underwear, and some ink pens. None of this stuff mattered to her. She grabbed the pictures of her kids and her degree off the wall before exiting the building never return there again.

Wednesday afternoon, Whitley spent the entire day cleaning up the house.

She took out the trash once she had finished. The day was May 24, 2000.

All of a sudden an unknown white van slowed down at the curb, right where she stood. All at once the door opened, someone grabbed her by the arm, and tossed her in.

The van sped down the street, with a terrified Whitley inside.

CHAPTER 2

Money, men and making love

Gena Moore was the definition of ghetto fabulous.

She was pretty, curvy, and had the attitude of the next hood chick.

However, this was very surprising since she grew up with in a very well off family.

Her parents were wealthy, she attended the best schools, and never wanted for anything.

Today she was off work and getting ready to go see her son's father.

He was going to give her some money for their son but of course this would be after she gave him a little something.

Once the babysitter arrived she paid her and headed to the other side of town.

Dominic was this gorgeous dude from the Islands. He was half Dominican and half Jamaican.

But he was raised in the states, so he didn't have an accent.

Gena met him a few years ago at a night club.

He bought her a drink and she gave him her number. They ended up in her bed that same night. 11 months later she gave birth to a gorgeous baby boy.

At first things were great. Then one day he decided that they were moving too fast and he told her he needed his space. Now they were just friends with benefits.

After a few drinks they got down to business. Gena made sure to have him wanting for more. When they finally finished up,

he reached into his pocket and took out a wad of money. Gena counted it as soon as he put it in her hand.

"65 dollars?" she asked him.

"Yeah, that's all I got right now."

"I drove all the way over here for some sixty-five funky dollars? That was my damn gas money to get over here Don."

"Shit I aint getting that many hours at work, plus I got other kids to take care of too man."

"Ooh you make me so damn sick! I should have stayed my black ass at home for all of this" she went off.

"What the hell do you want me to do huh? That little ten an hour aint doing shit for me, but let me take my ass back in the streets and get locked up again then Ima hear yo mouth again. I can't win with you" he said to her.

"But it aint like I ask you for money every day or even every week.

The only time I ask you for money is when I am desperate and really have to so don't try it. And when I first got wit you all you could do was brag about money you had, then as soon as I got with you all that money disappeared."

The next day Gena was exhausted once she got home from work.

She checked on the kids, Camrey was out. Tyshawn and Jermarcus were asleep as well.

Since Camrey was 12, Gena often let her watch her younger brothers when she couldn't afford a sitter.

However, she knew her boys were a handful, that's why she tried to get someone most of the times.

After taking her shower, Gena got comfortable on the sofa before deciding to call her boyfriend Irving over. He was far from her type, but it was more than his looks.

He made her feel good in more than one way. After a while, his looks stopped mattering to her.

He came in as she cleaned up her bedroom. She smiled as he smacked her on her butt.

"What's going on with cha?" he said as they kissed each other.

"I am good just got home from work. What you been doing all day?"

"Making this money, where the kids at?"

"They are all knocked out that after school must have worn em out."

"OK, lock the door so I can light one up real quick."

He sat on her bed and pulled out a dime bag.

Gena's eyes lit up like Christmas lights. She wasn't a big smoker, but after working so hard she needed something to relax her body.

Once they were high as the clouds they laid back in the bed.

"Oh yeah that was good." she chuckled.

"My boo high as hell" he laughed.

"Yeah, today at work some old white guy tried to steal a 6 pack of beer. He came to the counter with this funny stomach and before he could walk out of the store it fell out of his shirt" she explained to him.

"Damn Pops was trying to get his buzz on for real though."

"Yesterday I went to see my baby's father and this fool gave me 65 dollars like that was supposed to help me out."

"Why are you asking him for money anyways?"

"Because my baby needed some pampers and it's his responsibility to help me with him."

"A nigga aint trying to give up nothing unless you are too, so what chu do for em?"

"What? So you think I get down like that? I didn't give him a damn thing" she lied.

After some good loving Gena got ready for bed.

Irving on the other hand had somethings on his mind. They were good together and he loved Gena so much. A year ago when they met at the K-mart, he knew he had to have her. He gave her a few compliments then he showed up there when she got off work. From that night on they were together.

Irving was OK looking, he weighed in at 170 pounds,

dark skin he wore a low haircut, a nice smile, and he worked for a delivery company.

She knew he sold weed on the side and even though he was super sweet to her, she was not in the least attracted to him at first. And she would never have his baby. All of her children had handsome fathers and he wasn't close to that.

"Aye you still up Ma?" he asked her.

"Yeah I am, what do you want?" she replied.

"I care about you a lot, and you know that. I know you get tired of working all them hours all the times and I wanna help you any way I can."

"How are you gonna do that?"

"Could I move in, sale a few bags out of yo house and split it down the middle wit' you?"

"I don't want that stuff around my kids."

"And it won't be, I swear they won't even know."

"Well since I need the money that bad... I guess you can for a while."

2 weeks later, Irving moved in and gave Gena a stack of money.

"This looks like at least 2 grands in here" she said looking at it.

"Try 2500, and it's all yours. It's just my way of saying thank you."

"Come here" she said then she swallowed his tongue.

In a matter of days Irving's money doubled. Most people thought she was the candy lady, so it worked out well.

"2788..2789 dollars, I haven't seen this much money since I graduated high school"

Gena said as she counted today's earnings for her man.

"It's all yours too, I told you I had yo back" he said smiling.

"I can quit my job at K-mart and work part-time at the gas station now."

"Yeah, I told you all you had to do was give me a minute."

The next day Irving took her shopping. She got a new couch set, brand new beds for the kids, a desktop computer, and bedroom suit for her bedroom. The apartment looked like a lavish condo once they were finished.

Monday after work, Gena picked the kids up from school and then went home. She yawned as she unlocked the front door.

The kids walked in first. As she turned on the lights, Gena couldn't believe her eyes. Irving was in the bed with not one but 2 other women.

He hopped out of bed when he saw her. She screamed and started throwing whatever she could get her hands on at him.

"Let me explain, I promise this aint what it looks like." Irving told her.

"Get your shit and these hoes out of my house and don't you ever bring your cheating ass back here!"

"Will you just let me explain myself to you?"

"You wanna explain? OK give me one minute."

Gena walked over to her closet and slung the door open.

She pulled down a white shoe box and took the gun out of it.

Irving was so scared that he left without getting his clothes or shoes.

After snatching off the dirty sheets, Gena sat on the bed and lit up a blunt. She had to get the stress off of her mind.

A few days passed and Gena started to miss Irving and his money. But she knew he was bad for her. Besides her children needed her and she knew they would never hurt her the way a no-good man had.

On her off day she decided to pick the kids up from school and daycare.

"Cam how was school?" Gena asked her oldest and only daughter.

"It was OK, I got invited to my friend's birthday party this Saturday" the 12-year-old answered her mother.

"Maybe you'll get a chance to go if your chores are done all week."

"OK"

"Shawn how are you?"

"I'm fine, I have to do a math project on the computer tonight" Teyshawn told his mother.

He was a very handsome 9-year-old. Gena met his father 10 years ago at the bank. She thought he was the finest white man she had ever laid eyes on. So after opening a new bank account,

she also opened her legs to him. Since he was married, but separated they were only able to see each other every other week. He spoiled her with long vacations, expensive jewelry, 5-star restaurants and hotels.

After 6 months Gena became pregnant. When she broke the news to her lover he broke her heart and told her that their relationship had to end. But he was a great man and he sent her 1000 dollars once every few months for his son. Teyshawn had his father's straight black hair, his small lips and his height. At only 9 the boy was already 5 ft 3 inches tall. And all the little girls loved him.

On the other hand, Camrey was Gena's heart.

She met her father back in college. His name was Cameron, he was short for most guys but a sexy little man. He was light skinned,

about 5 ft 9 inches tall, had curly hair and he was studying to become a film director. They had 2 classes together. One night he ran into her at a house party. In no time they were a couple and Gena fell madly in love with him. No guy had ever made her feel the way he had.

Cameron adored her and they even planned on getting married after graduation.

On Thanksgiving break, Gena went home for a week.

After being really sick, her parents took her to the hospital. They found out she was pregnant. Her parents were so upset that they told her to marry the father or leave their home and never return. Gena explained to her parents that she was only 18 and not ready for such a commitment.

Once she got back to school she got some more horrible news. Cameron had been shot to death at a house party just the night before.

She had doubts about having an abortion, but after hearing the news about Cameron, she knew she had to keep her baby. Her child was the only part of him

that was left behind. So Gena left school after the first semester, got a full time job, her own place and waited for the arrival of her unborn child.

It was after 4pm when Gena pulled up into the complex.

The kids got out of the car and ran up to their building. After getting her things out of the car,

she got out and took her key out of her purse. The kids walked in before she did. Camrey turned on the lights and they all got a big surprise.

"What in the hell?" Gena said out loud.

All of their furniture was gone. She walked all over the house and sure enough, everything was gone.

All that was left were some of the kids clothes and some hangers. Gena ran to her phone and called Irving.

"Did you come into my house and steal my shit?" she asked him.

"No, I aint been over there since you kicked me out but do you..."

Before he could finish, Gena had ended the call.

"We are not staying here, let's go.. get your bags and let's go!"

she told her kids. They did what they were told and left out of the house.

They went to McDonald's for dinner that night. Gena did some thinking, it was really taking a toll on her. The money she had made from Irving was now gone and so was all of their things. Plus she quit her 2nd job so that meant they were in a bigger hole than before. Her kids had to have somewhere to sleep but there wasn't any way they would go back to that horrible apartment.

She would call the police the next morning. A tear rolled down her face.

She wiped it as Camrey walked back over to the table.

"Mom, what's the matter?" Camrey asked her mother.

"I'm alright baby.. sometimes us grown-ups cry, we get scared too.

And right now Mommy is really scared."

"Is it because our house got robbed?"

"That and then some... but that is nothing for you to worry about all right?

Go play with your brothers and be a kid. Let me worry about the grown-up stuff."

"OK"

Gena watched as her daughter ran back over to the play area.

After leaving the restaurant, Gena took the kids back to the apartment. She turned on the lights hoping all their stuff would have magically returned. But it was still as empty as it was the first time.

"Go into your rooms and get out an outfit for school.

Camrey help Shawn pick out something and hurry so we can go" Gena told her kids.

"Where are we going? "Teyshawn asked his mother.

"We are going to a hotel for the night. Hurry up so we can get out of here."

Then there was a knock at the door. Gena opened the door and rolled her eyes. There stood Irving. He was the last person that she wanted to see right now.

"What are you doing here? I told you they took everything so there is nothing here that belongs to you." she informed him.

"Can I holla at chu for a minute?"

She followed him outside on the porch. Gena sighed before she gave him the chance to speak.

"I wanted to apologize to you about that shit that went down a couple days ago.

I got comfortable and I took advantage of the situation. I didn't mean to have them in yo crib like that.

And I swear on everything I didn't have nothing to do with the whole robbery. But I can find out who was behind it. And I know you need some help. Here, this should cover a few things that you lost"

he said handing her a wad of money.

She looked down to see at least 7 hundred-dollar bills.

"Thank you, I gotta help them get ready."

"That's cool, I still love you and we'll talk about this later on."

"OK, bye"

The next day, it was May 24, 2001. Gena almost didn't wake up and go to work.

But the mother in her knew she had to so that her kids could eat and have a roof over their heads.

Since they stayed the night at a hotel she had to wake them up extra early to drop them off at school.

Then she would come back to the hotel and get ready for work.

Gena sighed as she looked into the mirror. She had just showered and put on her uniform for work. Things were falling apart, and she didn't know just how much more she could take. Irving had cheated on her, their apartment had been robbed, and now she didn't even know where they would stay for the night. The hotel was 150 dollars per night. There was no way she could afford that. After putting her purse onto her shoulder, she turned off the lights and headed out of the door. As she unlocked her car door, this unknown white van pulled up beside her and the door opened. Someone snatched her inside and then sped off.

CHAPTER 3

The not so perfect Shantale

"See love covers all sins. We got people around here hating one another because of looks, money, cars,

and houses. But we are all one in the body of Christ. I dare you to love that child that gets sent to the principal office every day. I dare you to love that husband that lost his third job this year and can't afford to take you on that cruise you have been planning on going on for the last 2 years. I double dog dare you to love that neighbor or family member that has that Mercedes or BMW that you have been working 2 jobs trying to afford. Or that friend who has a three story house with the swimming pool in the back yard. Somebody turn to your neighbor and say "I dare you to love em" somebody shout hallelujah in this place this morning!" Pastor Toris Atkins preached.

The church was on fire and you could feel God's presence in the place.

This was a normal Sunday morning at Galilee Baptist Church, and he had brought the gospel in such a way, every single week. Sweat dripped down his face as he walked the floor and preached.

At only 35 years old, Toris was the Bishop and full of the anointing.

The church was filled with over two hundred members weekly.

People were up shouting, clapping, and praising God. Shantale Atkins, was his wife and first lady. She was standing on her feet with her right hand up showing off her freshly manicured nails. She was speaking in tongues and shaking her head.

"Matthew 22:39 says, *And the second is like it, you shall love your neighbor as you love yourself.* So when you see that neighbor going without don't turn your back on them. Do what you can to help them. Let me ask you this, where would we be if Jesus turned his back on us? Lord I need my bills paid and Jesus says, Darn I sure hate to hear that, but I'll pray for you. That's how we as so called Christians are today. Get your love walk right with God! Time is not gonna wait on you!" Toris went on to say.

After most of the members left, Shantale joined her husband in his office.

"That was some sermon you put on today Bishop." she told him.

"Hey there Beautiful, I saw you getting your praise on today." Toris smiled as

he as he took off his robe.

"Yeah, I had to, God has been too good to me."

"Right on... are you ready to go to dinner?"

"I am"

He grabbed his bible and took her by the hand.

Most couples would envy them. They were two beautiful black people who had great careers, money to do any and everything they could imagine, and they were deeply in love. It had been 8 years ago when they got married and it still felt like it was the honeymoon. Shantale had a gorgeous light brown complexion, she was a perfect size 10, and she wore her hair cut like Nia Long did in the movie *Best Man*.

And a lot of people said she looked like actress Essence Atkins from TV show *Half and Half*.

"We have to be at Reverend Bullock's church by 4 today, they are having his

Anniversary program" Toris informed his wife.

"Oh that was today, we need to go shower, dinner, and then head over that way."

"You're right about that, I sweat so much, felt like I was getting baptized again."

Shantale couldn't stop herself from laughing. She knew that her husband had a sense of humor, but he was even funnier when he was serious.

"Come on Mr. Funny man and let's go eat before these restaurants get too packed" Shantale said putting her arm into his arm.

He opened the door and they headed out to the car.

Monday morning, Toris came downstairs a little after seven that morning.

He kissed his wife and poured himself a cup of coffee.

Shantale placed their breakfast on the table. Today on the menu, they were having turkey sausage links, eggs and blueberry muffins. He blessed the food before they ate.

"Another day's journey, are you ready for your many high school students and their problems?"

Toris quizzed his wife.

She was a high school guidance counselor, and he was a psychologist with his own practice.

"Well I try to go in every morning with an opened mind.

The graduation test are coming up and I am more nervous than the students. Those things are evil. I have seen brilliant children that have been on the honor roll since elementary school not able to graduate because of those test. I wish I could band them myself." Shantale expressed.

"I rebuke those test in the name of Jesus right now!" Toris shouted.

Shantale laughed so hard that she spit out her orange juice.

He laughed as she wiped her mouth and then the table.

"Stop it, you are so silly" she chuckled.

"You know I love seeing that beautiful smile."

She couldn't help but blush he always knew exactly what to say to her.

Once Shantale got to her office there was already a line of students awaiting her arrival. She unlocked her door and called in the first student.

"What's your student id number?" Shantale asked her.

"Its 6732" the girl softly replied.

"Vintrice... how may I help you this morning?"

The girl was dark skinned, very petite, pretty, and her hair was done in these small light brown micro braids. She was wearing a designer t shirt, a pair of hip hugger jeans and some cute pink and white sneakers.

Her grades popped up on her computer screen. Shantale was suddenly

disappointed and wanted some answers right away.

"What's going on with your grades? You are a senior correct?"

"Yes, I got pregnant earlier this year and my mom said that I have to get my own place once the baby comes. I started working so I could move on my own but I can't work and do my schoolwork too." the girl explained.

"I don't think dropping out of school is the best option for you or your baby. Could you try working a later shift? There are grants out there that will pay for you to go to school, and childcare for your child once it's born. You are too bright of a girl to settle. Come see me after school and we will work something out."

A smile appeared on the girl's face.

"Thank you so much Mrs. Atkins."

"You're welcome, get to class, and take this excuse."

Toris came home to find his wife busy in the kitchen after work. He kissed her on the cheek and then sat at the bar.

"How was your day?" she asked him.

"I had an all right day. I have this bad headache... I am a man of God, but I am human as well" he replied.

"What's wrong, why did you say that?"

"This guy Johnathan, I have been seeing him for about 6 weeks. He has been gay since he was 13 years old and wants to come out of the closet. And he asked me how should he tell his family."

"Oh lord, what did you say to him?"

"I told him that he should sit them down... but the more I spoke, the more I got conflicted in my spirit. So I told him that our father makes no mistakes and he was not born that way. That is just a strategy that the enemy used to keep him separated from God... I told him that he needed to allow God in to change his desires. Psalm 37:4 says, *Delight thyself in the Lord; and he shall give thee the desires of thine heart.* People think by hearing that verse all they have to do is pray, fast and read the word and God will bless them with everything their heart desires. No that scripture means if you abide in me, seek after me then I will change your desires and give you the desires I have for your life. This young man needs to seek the father and his plans for his life. The desires he possess are not of the father. Just as a man who is an adulterer, or a drunker, or anything that separates us from God is unholy."

"Did you really say that to him?"

"Of course I did, he told me I was supposed to tell him what he wanted to hear and not what he needed to hear since he was paying me 150 dollars an hour. Then he got up and walked out of the room."

"Well speaking as your wife and a human being...

you have to give them your educated opinion and your wisdom from God.

But being gay isn't something people can just shake off. He is the one who has to deal with God on that, not you. So if you feel like you can't tell your clients the truth without taking it personal, you may need to rethink your career. If I paid you to give me professional advice I would want just that. Sure some people can handle the truth but most cant" Shantale explained to her husband.

"I must say that even I can take correction. That was some wise words for me thank you baby."

"And see you didn't even have to pay for that."

He couldn't help but laugh at her comment.

Shantale held women's bible study on Wednesday night.

She always held it in the basement of their house.

Toris turned it into a classroom and lounge, it was a very nice area once he finished it.

"Good evening ladies, I hope you all have had a blessed week thus far. Tonight we are gonna hit a very juicy subject." Shantale said to her class.

Then she took a dry eraser maker and wrote on the whiteboard.

It was 25 women in the class, and they loved her bible studies.

She wrote the words *True love* on the board.

"Now I know you all are probably wondering why I chose those 2 words to base tonight's bible study on. But some of us have been with so many wrong men that we feel like all men are dogs. Or you thought he was the one until you married him. Well I am a witness; true love does exist." Shantale said to her class.

The women nodded their heads some even said amen.

"Let's turn to Proverbs 18:22 and see what God has to say about love. And it reads, ***"he who finds a wife finds a good thing and obtains the favor from God"***.

So does that mean because I am 45 and still single I'm supposed to go out and help God find me somebody?" Shantale quizzed the ladies.

They all shook their heads saying no.

"God does everything in due time. Just because you see someone with the perfect relationship that doesn't mean it won't happen for you. Maybe you need growing in a certain area that God is trying to deliver you in. Or maybe he is getting that mate he has for you ready."

Sister Vanessa raised her hand. She was 36, single, heavy set, yet very beautiful.

"Why is it wrong to have sex with the man that you know you want to marry one day? I mean how do you know you'll like the sex after the wedding if you aint even tried him out yet?" She asked the first lady.

All of the women fell over laughing.

"Wait a minute.. OK I have an answer for that one." Shantale chuckled.

She flipped through her bible until she got to the right chapter.

"Peter 1:15 says, *"but as he who called you is holy, you also be holy in all your conduct"*. Jesus didn't walk on this earth screwing every woman he came in contact with. So if Jesus can go without sex for 33 years why can't we do the same? Or at least wait until after marriage?"

"Jesus did a lot of things that I couldn't do. So try again" Vanessa replied.

Shantale found herself laughing after the class dismissed. They ended up having this ongoing debate just off the night's lesson, talk about an hot topic.

Just as Shantale headed up the stairs to retire for the night, the doorbell rang.

She turned around and headed to the door. When she opened it up, she smiled. There stood her baby sister and her newborn baby boy.

"Oh my Lord! What a surprise, get in here" she cried.

They gave each other a hug before going into the living room.

"Well Aiden turned a month-old today, so we decided to get out of the house. He hasn't been out since I brought him home from the hospital" Angelica said as she took the baby out of his car seat.

He was a handsome baby boy with the most gorgeous skin tone and hair.

"Look at my nephew, he is a doll" Shantale smiled.

"Do you wanna hold em?"

"Sure"

Angelica gave her the baby. He snuggled close to his aunt as if he knew exactly who she was.

"He likes you... what are you waiting on to have me some nieces and nephews?"

"Toris is always so busy with the church and I am with school and church. After the first

5 years I gave up on the dream."

"As long as mother nature still visits you each month you can still have kids."

"I love kids and I have so much love to give, but I would have to put my whole life on hold and I can't do that right now."

"Well I thought the same until I had this one and its hard work I won't lie. But, Sis its so worth it."

Angelica and baby Aiden stayed for a about an hour. Shantale gave them hugs and walked them out to the car.

Toris was sleeping peacefully that night, until he started having this horrible nightmare.

Shantale ran up the stairs and hid this black bag into the bathroom cabinet.

A woman in all black followed her into the room. Shantale screamed and held her hands up.

"Stay away from me you freak!" Shantale yelled at her.

"Tell him the truth or I will my child" the lady in black said to her.

Toris came into the room to see what the commotion was all about.

"Shan what's all the noise all about?" he asked them.

"I am your angel Toris... your wife is hiding a dark secret from you. Tell him or I will" The old woman warned her.

"What are you talking about?" Toris asked her.

Shantale ran over to her husband and wrapped her arms around his waist.

Then she looked up at him.

"Baby she is some crazy old lady that followed me home. I don't have any idea why she is here. But whatever you do don't listen to her."

"I will be back tell him now my dear."

Shantale ran over to the closet and pulled out a gun and fired 4 shots at the woman.

They watched as the woman fell to the floor in a puddle of blood.

"What is wrong with you?! You just killed an innocent person! What are you hiding from me? Tell me now or I will blow your brains out myself."

"Toris... please don't do this to me" Shantale started to cry.

Then she pointed the gun at her own self.

She was crying so hard that she could barely see.

He rushed over to her and tried to take the gun out of her hand.

Out of nowhere a gun shot went off. Toris looked down to see blood coming from his wife's stomach.

"Baby what did you do" Toris yelled?!

Toris suddenly woke up in a cold sweat. Shantale woke up as well.

"What is wrong with you? Why did you wake up like that?" Shantale asked half asleep.

"I had a nightmare...would you ever hide something from me?" he asked her.

"Where did that come from?"

"I had a dream that you were hiding a deep dark secret from me and you shot yourself just so I wouldn't find out about it."

KARMA IS A MOTHA

Shantale felt this guilt go all over here. She knew God was telling him something in that dream, it was mostly due to the fact that she really was hiding a deep dark secret from him.

And this secret could destroy their marriage. Shantale knew he could never find out about it. So far she had done a good job at hiding it from him.

But what's done in the dark always comes to the light.

Growing up she and Angelica lived the best that life could offer. Her mother had spent her teen years and most of her early twenties in Paris France as a super model. Her father was a bass player for a successful jazz band. However, their perfect lives soon ended when Shantale was only ten years. Her father had been killed while on the road touring.

He left them over 5 million dollars in insurance money. Their mother took the loss really hard and started doing drugs. The money left quickly, and by the time Shantale graduated from high school, they had to file bankruptcy. There was no way Shantale could go to college without a scholarship. One day while hanging out, she ran into an old classmate. The former friend told Shan how good life had been for her since graduating. Then she told her about her new, good paying job. The job turned out to be stripping at a popular strip club in town.

Shantale decided to do it just to pay for school. The money turned out to be so good that she was even able to send money home for her baby sister. She was also able to use some of the money she made from stripping to help her mother pay down some of her debt she accumulated during her drug use.

"No, I would never keep a secret from you." she lied to him.

"OK. I'm sorry I woke you, let's go back to bed love."

He kissed her cheek and then laid back down.

Shantale couldn't sleep after hearing about Toris' dream. He was really a man of God.

She didn't want to hide things from him, but how would he accept her for keeping such a lie from him? It was as if their entire relationship had been built on a lie.

Angelica called her to have lunch the next afternoon. They were outside on the patio at one of their favorite restaurants. Shantale was very quiet. She had a lot on her mind, then Angelica finally decided to speak on it.

"What is up with the silence and long face?" she asked her older sister.

"Last night Toris wakes up in a cold sweat. He said he had a nightmare about me. In the dream I was hiding a deep dark secret from him and I shot myself just to keep him from finding out what it was," Shantale confessed.

"What has you so uneasy about that?" Angelica asked next.

She figured Shantale told her husband about stripping a long time ago.

"He doesn't know about college and how I paid for it." she came clean.

"You mean he doesn't know that you used to strip to pay for your tuition?"

"No, when we met he swept me off my feet. I couldn't tell a man of God I stripped to send myself to college. He would think I was some kind of slut or something and I love my man too much to lose him."

"I am sure that if he found out he would forgive you and let that be the past. It's not like you did it after you guys got married or anything."

"Well no, but I portrayed myself to be someone totally different than who I really was."

"If you had to pretend to be someone that you really wasn't then he wasn't the one for you."

"He is the one for me. No man completes me the way he does. We are meant to be."

"I think you should tell him; how would you feel if he kept a secret from you?"

"I can't tell him, he thinks Victoria Secret models are sluts, I wouldn't stand a chance."

"You will never know until you tell him. If anyone knows about forgiveness its him."

"That's fine but this is one that I'm gonna take to the grave."

She took a 20 dollar bill out of her purse then laid it on the table.

Sunday a youth minister preached the sermon. He did a good job, but he didn't have the church on fire as Toris usually did. The annual church revival was coming up and he was saving himself for that. After church was let out, Toris and Shantale went out to greet the members. The members all loved their pastor, some weren't too key on Shantale though. And it was simply because they wanted to be Mrs. Bishop Toris Atkins.

A young man walked over to Toris as he and Shantale headed to the car. He was slim, dark skinned, had on some sneakers,

and baggy jeans. He looked Shantale up and down and then he looked at Bishop.

"Bishop good afternoon, my name is Jeffery Nixon, I was riding through... and something told me to stop in. I got a lot out of the sermon" the man told Toris.

"I'm glad to hear that, these church doors are always opened." Toris smiled.

Then Jeffery looked at Shantale once more.

Toris caught his eye so he decided to do what a real man would do.

"Oh, this is my wife, Shantale Atkins." he introduced her to the visitor.

"Hello, it's nice to meet you." Shantale said shaking his hand.

He softly kissed her hand.

"You are a very beautiful woman, where have I met you before?" he asked her.

"I'm sorry, I don't believe we ever have." Shantale said feeling sort of uncomfortable.

Jeffery started snapping his fingers then he smiled.

"Oh yeah, you used to strip at the Regal." he reminded her.

"No you have me mistaken for someone else sir" Shantale said again shaking her head. She said a quick prayer to God. She wanted this guy to leave and fast before he said something that could ruin her entire life.

"Yeah, you used to be the main event. I used to get a lap dance from you every Friday night your name was uh... Spice. Damn you are a lucky man Rev" Jeffery said hitting Toris on the shoulder.

"Sir, you must think I am someone else." Shantale said grabbing Toris' hand so she could indicate she was ready to go.

"I don't forget faces... you got a tattoo on yo left thigh of a snake wrapped around a rose" the man continued.

Toris' heart stopped beating for a second. This man was right, his wife did have that exact tattoo on her thigh. She told him she got it when she turned twenty-one as a reminder that she was finally free from her strict parents.

Toris slid his hand from her grip and then looked at the man.

"Excuse me, I have to go lock up my office. It was nice meeting you Jeff, don't let this be your last time coming." he said shaking his hand once more.

Then he walked away from the two of them.

Shantale rolled her eyes and then walked over to their car.

The ride home was hell. She knew he was mad beyond at her.

He couldn't fathom the idea that his sweet innocent wife once shook her ass for money.

It was so degrading, so careless, and only a woman with no self-esteem would do such a thing. Then there was the church, what would they say if word got around? He could hear the concerns, letters, and emails now.

She followed him up to their bedroom once they got to the house.

"Toris I am soooo sorry. I never meant to keep that from you. And I had a good reason why I chose to strip anyways," Shantale replied.

He didn't say a word to her, he undid his tie and unbutton his shirt.

"Toris, it's just when I fell in love with you..."

"You told me you came from a very strict and religious home. You said you didn't even know who Usher was." Toris interrupted her.

"I know, but I..."

"Don't even try to explain it. Get the heck out of my house!"

"Please hear me out Baby." she tried to hold back the tears.

He rolled his eyes at her and then walked out of the room.

Shantale rushed over to her closet and pulled out her suitcase. She couldn't hold back the tears. She fell to the floor and cried until she fell asleep against the wall.

Once she woke up she packed a week's worth of clothes and then left for a hotel.

Friday night came. Shantale got dressed up in this astonishing lavender sundress, she curled her hair,

did her make up, and then drove to the church for the last night of the revival.

It was May 24, 2002. Instead of sitting on the front pew as she usually did, tonight Shantale decided to sit in the middle of the church. Sure enough it was a house full. People often drove from miles away to get the gospel from Mr. Atkins.

Toris stood as the choir finished their selection.

"Let the church say amen... say amen again. It's a blessing to in the house of the Lord one more time. This revival has done exactly what it was supposed to have done and that's revive the soul... Saints I must tell you, the devil has been after me this week. I have been tried in the worst way.

But in front of everyone here I wanna say Satan I rebuke you in the name of Jesus you have no power here so flee right now!" Toris shouted.

His congregation started clapping and praising God right away.

He wiped his handsome brown face with a hand towel and then opened his bible.

"I had a lot of thought about not doing my sermon tonight. But God is still in control.

Turn to your neighbor and say neighbor God is still in control".

Shantale closed her eyes and said a quick prayer to the man upstairs.

"I was going to preach about being revived, and how to heal the soul. But tonight God has led me to a different subject. Let's turn to Romans 13:11- 13...it reads... *And that, knowing the time, that now it is high time to awake out of sleep: for now our salvation nearer than when we believed. The night is far spent, the day is at hand: let us therefore cast off the works of darkness and let us put on the armor of light. Let us walk properly as in the day, not revelry and drunkenness, not in lewdness and lust, not in strife and envy.* You may be seated" Toris spoke to the church.

Everyone closed their bibles and took their seats.

"Some of us are walking around blind, deaf, and ignorant to the word of God.

We go to church and leave the same way that we came in. And that's not the purpose for church. We come here to get the true knowledge of Christ. We come here to praise God for the countless things he has done for us. We come to fellowship with our brothers and sisters in Christ. But some of us come to just get out of the house. Some come because we grew up being brought to church. I'm here to tell you wake up and smell the frankincense. You are walking in darkness, and it isn't gonna get you any closer to God. Some of these pastors have fooled you,

made you believe all you had to do was come to church and God would handle the rest. And I'm here to tell you, Get out of Darkness! Read your bible, pray, fast, and come to church to get a better understanding. There is an old saying *how can the blind lead the blind?* and I agree how can we as pastors lead people to Christ when we are still smoking, drinking, sleeping with our members and going to clubs more than the Dee-jays" Toris preached.

He was walking the floor and sweating from his head down to his neck. People started standing up and shaking their heads. It was incredible how anointed and wise he was.

"Y'all don't hear me tonight! Its time out for secrets, its time out for lies, God is ready to show up and show out" He went on to say.

Shantale couldn't take being there a minute longer. He was preaching directly to her and she was the only one who knew so. Before she could let the tears fall from her eyes,

she excused herself from the pew and hurried out of the exit. She went out to her car and unlocked the door. Tears poured from her eyes. How could her perfect life be falling apart all of a sudden?

She got into the car and drove to the hotel. After changing her clothes she went down to the bar and ordered a stiff drink. Angelica called while she was taking a sip from the drink.

Ever since Toris asked her to leave, she hadn't spoken to anyone.

She finally picked up the phone and by that time Angelica had hung up. Then she saw that she left her a voice message. Shantale played the message back.

"Hey, Shan it's me once again. Now I am starting to worry. I went by the house earlier today, and Toris said you were gone once again. I know you don't go out that much. Did he do away with your body and I don't know anything about it? Please give me a call as soon as possible. I wanna know if you told him the truth yet." Angelica said in the voice message.

Shantale looked at the phone and pressed 7 to erase the message. She didn't want to speak with anyone but Toris. He hurt her so bad when he told her he to get out of their home. True he did pay the mortgage, but it was just as much her house as it was his.

And the way he looked at her, it was as if he hated her guts.

He didn't even try to hear her point of view. It seemed like he was no longer the sweet humble Toris she

fell in love with back in college. She needed a plan and one fast. What could she do to get him to love her again?

After a couple drinks, Shantale went out to her car to get her suitcase out of the backseat. Out of nowhere a white van pulled up beside her and grabbed her by the arm. They were down the street with a frightened Shantale before she could even make a sound.

CHAPTER 4

Welcome to Hell

Shantale started screaming uncontrollably as the man wrapped duct tape around her legs, hands, and mouth. Her body was shaking, sweat started to drip from her face. Scared would have been an understatement to describe how she felt.

"Calm down little lady, the fun has just begun." the man chuckled.

He was wearing a ski mask, and all black attire.

Once he had her tied up pretty good, he laid her on her back and she rode that way for over 5 hours. When the van finally came to a stop, the man carried her inside this beautiful house and then he pushed her down a flight of stairs.

It knocked her out cold for hours. When she did come to,

she was sitting at this table along with two other women. They looked as if they had been there for a long time. Their hair looked horrible and their skin looked dry and stale.

Out of nowhere a woman appeared in front of them. She was wearing a mask over her face and all black attire as well. She was slim about 135 pounds, 5 ft 7 inches tall and looked like she worked out quite a bit.

"I would like to welcome our last guest, Shantale Atkins to our little party. You 3 women are heartless, cruel, and snobby. And it is my job to give you a taste of your own medicine. One of you had the world. A good man, beautiful kids, and a great career. But that wasn't enough was it? So you had to be trifling and start screwing your boss. So after a while he threw you away like yesterday's newspaper. Your husband found out and took your kids from you and left you broke and lonely.

Next we have *Miss anybody can get it*. She had a baby in college so her parents disowned her. Then she had to work 2 jobs to take care of them 3 kids, that all have different daddies. I mean do your legs automatically open every time a man comes by? And last but not least we have *Ms. Holier than thou*. Your father was killed when you were ten and your mother couldn't live without him. So she started doing drugs to cope with his lost. She must have been really lonely to spend over 5 million dollars up on crack. By the time you graduated high school y'all were in bankruptcy. So to pay for college you had to do something strange for a little piece of change. Then the man of your dreams came along, and you made him think you were this innocent perfect little lady. He married you and made you the first lady at Galilee Baptist. That didn't last long because one of your old customers came by and told Bishop just how perfect his little wife really was. He kicked you out and never looked back again. There is a saying *what goes around goes around*.

And my ladies I believe this is your time. Welcome to hell," she said followed by this devious laughter, then she walked back up the stairs.

Shantale looked over at the other 2 women. She couldn't believe her eyes,

she knew these women a little too well. They had all been best friends back in grammar school all the way up until high school graduation.

"Whitley, Gena is that you?" Shantale asked the other women.

"Yeah, it's us all right, it's been what 13 years?" Gena asked.

"Yeah, too long... how long have y'all even been here?" Shantale questioned the ladies next.

"It's been 2 years yesterday for me." Whitley said as if she could barely speak.

"A year yesterday for me" Gena replied next.

"Oh my god how is she able to do that?! I would die first before I stayed here that long. Who is she and why does she want to destroy us? And how does she even know about our lives?"

Shantale went on and on trying not to panic.

"Calm down, whoever the scank is she is smart. She turned all of our family and friends against us so once we came up missing they wouldn't care." Gena schooled her girls.

"But how does she even know us? Who did we hurt bad enough that would literally kidnap us? "

Shantale asked next.

"A lot of people" Whitley said holding her head down.

This was so surprising to see her this way. In school she was always so gorgeous, smart, well dressed, and always had something to say. Now she was really quiet, she looked homeless, and in the need of a serious bath.

Being there for the last two years had really taken a tow on her. She had hurt so many people including her own parents. Then she hurt her husband and their kids. Why couldn't she just except what God gave her and be content with it? No she had to have her cake and eat it too.

Then out of nowhere the woman ran downstairs. She slapped them as hard as she could.

"Who in the hell told either one of you that you could say a word?! I don't think I did so shut up! No one speaks unless spoken to first, do I make myself clear!" she yelled.

They all nodded their heads yes.

Whitley burst into tears; she had had enough of this.

"Who are you and why are you doing this to us?!

Haven't you tortured us enough?!" Whitley shouted out.

The woman walked over to her and slapped spit out of her mouth.

"Didn't I tell your yellow ass to shut up?! You women have destroyed people's lives all of your damn lives. Now it's my turn to destroy you. So sit back and enjoy the ride." the woman started laughing.

Shantale felt the tears slide down her cheeks. There was no guarantee that they would even make it out of this place alive.

"I should kill each of you slowly. You three bitches made my life a living hell! I tried to kill myself on numerous occasions because of the things you used to do to me! I used to feel like I was nothing. But that shit stops today, right now! I am worth loving." the woman said holding back her tears.

Still they were all clueless and had no idea of who she really was.

However they did feel bad to know they almost caused someone to take their own life. Shantale, Whitley, or even Gena could never live with themselves if they caused someone to commit suicide.

2 weeks came and left by very slowly for Toris. He was in his office at the church going over his notes for Sunday's sermon.

It had been 2 weeks since he had heard from Shantale. Every time a church member or relative asked about her he had to make up a lie and say she was away on a retreat or on a business trip. But Angelica was coming by the house or calling every single day. She even surprised Toris by coming to church last Sunday. She was missing her sister just as much as he was missing his wife. But what could he tell her, he didn't have a clue himself? He picked up the picture of them. They were at the Potter's house and T.D Jakes had just gave one of his most powerful sermons. Shantale was wearing a stylish black and gold suit.

She had a gold flower in her hair as well. Since the day he met her he knew she was the most beautiful woman he had ever laid eyes on.

At once Toris imagined seeing Shantale on stage half naked and shaking her ass in front of a crowd full of horny men. Some were whistling at her, others yelled while throwing dollar bills onto the stage. Every time he had this thought it made him mad as hell. She was supposed to be his wife, a virtuous woman sent from heaven, not club Regal. How many of her customers did she do more than dance for them?

Then he pulled out his cell phone and called her phone.

"You have reached Mrs. Shantale Atkins, I am not available right now. Leave me a detailed message and

I promise to call you back. And remember God loves you and so do I" she said on her answering machine.

Instead of leaving a message, he just closed the phone and put it back into his pocket.

Where was his wife? There was so much they needed to figure out. They needed to work past this and have the amazing marriage they once had. He closed his eyes and looked toward heaven.

"Father God, I am asking you right now to bring my wife home to me. I forgive her and I ask that she forgives me for what I said to her. She is the only woman that I feel this way about.

Give us the strength to not hold any secrets back and go forward and not look back at this situation. I ask that it is done in the name of Jesus, amen."

He opened his eyes and stared at the blank wall. God was in control and if it was meant to be, Shantale would return home.

Camrey lied in the bed just thinking. It had been over a year since her mother left. And now they were living with the grandparents they never knew existed.

Gena always told her kids that her parents were dead, so they never talked about them. However they couldn't be because they had all kinds of pictures of Gena on the walls, in photo albums, and their mother looked a lot like these people. Sure Camrey and her little brothers had everything now from new sneakers, clothes, money,

toys, any food you could think of. But Camrey would give it all up just to have her mother back. No Gena was never mother of the year, but she was still their mother. And Camrey needed her more than ever.

Teyshawn and Jermarcus were very happy with their new found life.

They got to do any and everything a kid their ages wanted to do.

Camrey on the other hand stayed in her bedroom if she wasn't at school.

People kept telling her that Gena was dead. But deep down she didn't believe it.

Her mother was too strong to die so suddenly.

She was just taking some time off. After her boyfriend cheated on her and they robbed her home, Gena almost lost her mind.

Maybe she did need a break from this cruel cold world.

Kyle walked into the house after a long day from work.

2 years later he had been mother and father to his kids. There was only time for work, and the kids. He knew what Whitley did was horrible,

but she was still their mother. She could at least come visit them, or write them, or even call them. They talked about her every day and they really missed her.

Kylie was quiet one evening after school. Instead of watching her normal cartoons once they got home, she ran up to her bedroom. Kyle ran up to see what was going on with her.

"What's the matter Sunshine?" he asked her.

"I really miss her, why did she leave us? Did me and Jr do something wrong?" Kylie questioned her father.

"No, don't ever think that way. Your mother and I had some issues.

And I told her to not come around until she got herself together. You guys are very important to both of us, but right now your mom needs sometime alone." Kyle had to lie.

"It's been like 2 years, how much longer is it supposed to take?"

"When you have problems like that, it doesn't have a time frame."

"Would you ever leave us like that?"

"I would never leave you guys. And your mom didn't leave on purpose either."

Kylie was now 9 years old. She was growing up so fast and she was turning into a gorgeous young lady. She looked more and more like Whitley. He gave her a hug then they went downstairs to order a pizza.

CHAPTER 5

Plotting and Praying

Whitley couldn't sleep any that night, so she woke the girls up.

"What's wrong?" Shantale asked her friend.

"We have to figure out a way to get the hell out of here." Whitley said to them.

"I know that's the truth, enough is enough. I might kill that bitch for real once she lets us out of here," Gena said next.

7:05 am, the lady in the mask came down to check on her hostages.

"Oh what a beautiful day it is! You 3 look like some homeless crackheads" she laughed.

Gena rolled her eyes to keep her composure.

"It was my pleasure ruining your lives one by one.

Whitley I had a private eye set up a camera in the hotel room and Mr.

Dilland's office. Then I personally delivered each D.V.D. to you, Kyle,

and Dilland. Then Gena I had a few of my people rob your apartment and made you think Irving did it" the lady confessed.

"You Bitch! How dare you try to destroy me!" Gena exclaimed.

The woman ran over and punched blood from her mouth.

"I'd kick your raggedy ass if I wasn't tied down to this chair!

Let me up so I can kick your ass Baltimore style!" Gena screamed out.

"Gena, sweetie please...just be quiet. It's OK just calm down. It's gonna be all right." Shantale comforted her friend.

"You better listen to your friend. She was married to a bishop. So a little of his wisdom rubbed off on her. Praise the Lord Saints!" The lady mocked Shantale.

It took all the God in Shantale not to snap on her.

But it didn't work because she had to say something.

"You can't hold us down here forever. Somebody is gonna come looking for us." Shantale assured her kidnapper.

"Bitch please! I have had Whitley here for 2 years and Gena for over a year. I made sure your families would hate you so they wouldn't wanna find your sorry asses." she informed them.

"Well Bitch, you better go ahead and kill my ass. Because if I do get out of here alive your ass is good as grass. Don't take my word for it either," Gena spoke up.

"Oh trust me, that can be arranged."

Then she went up the stairs leaving them speechless once again.

Whitley looked at the other ladies and sighed.

"I am not giving up until I am out of here. This is insane and that freak is really taking us through it. I need to get to my kids." Whitley explained.

Gena stayed up all that night. There had to be a way out of this hell hole, and she wouldn't get a wink of sleep until she had it figured out.

After hours she finally had a plan. She woke the other 2 up and shared the details with them. Shantale said a quick prayer with them just to be on the safe side.

Ms. Lady came down the stairs around 8 that morning. The girls were in action ready for her. As soon as she was close enough, Gena jumped on top of her like a lion hopping on a deer in the jungle. The woman started screaming as Gena punched her face repeatedly. Then 2 huge men ran down and pulled her off of the woman.

Gena had the mask in her hand when they grabbed her.

"Dandra?" Gena asked in complete shock.

"Yeah, it's me, karma is a motha aint it?" she said standing to her feet.

Shantale was lost for words. Out of everyone in the world, Dandra was the one who had kidnapped them?

"You did this because we teased you a few times in school?" Shantale asked the lady.

"Bull shit! You three heifers tortured me throughout high school! Sticks and stones may break my bones, but words could never hurt me. Whoever came up with that saying was a liar. Yeah sticks and stones may break my bones, but they will heal one day. Your words have damaged me for a lifetime. So yeah I had to get even." Dandra explained.

The men tied Gena back to the table while she finished her speech.

Shantale was still in shock. She knew they had been really cruel to Dandra back in the day, but that was almost 15 years ago.

Gena even felt bad. Every time Dandra would pass them in the hall, it would be her who had something mean to say about her.

Whitley felt like dying, out of the 3 of them she had hurt Dandra the most. No one could forget how trifling she had been for doing what she did to the poor girl. It was beyond mean.

CHAPTER 6

15 years earlier

Whitley entered the cafeteria with her 2 best friends right behind her.

It was a Monday afternoon there at Downer high school.

No one was more popular than the three divas. Their parents were all rich, had class, and plenty of power. Back then Gena had long hair that hung down her shoulders. She wore tight jeans, and skits that were too short to be worn at any school. Shantale had her hair cut in a cute mushroom bob. All she wore back then were jeans, t-shirts, and sneakers. On the other hand Whitley wore her hair long and straight every day. She never wore anything but skirts and dresses.

They all wore make up and they wore it well.

The year was 1987 and Downer high was the school to attend.

As the girls walked over to the lunch line, this girl stood in front of them. She put the L-A in lame. Her clothes were so plain, her hair was combed back into a stale ponytail, and she was really skinny. Her name was Dandra Byrd. The only thing on her that was some what attractive was her golden skin tone. It was the color of caramel and it was so smooth.

"Oh my God, look at her shoes." Whitley chuckled to her friends.

"Wow, those are like so old. Them shoes were out when my grandma was in school. Hell she probably gave em to her." Gena laughed out loud.

"Y'all can be so mean. She is right in front of us.

What if she hears you?" Shantale said being the angel of the bunch.

Even before marrying Toris she tried to stay out of trouble.

It wasn't in her character to bad mouth innocent people.

Dandra looked down at her white, well they were once white Chuck Taylor sneakers. Ever since she first started Downer high back in the 9th grade, these 3 chicks had made her life a living hell.

Most of the kids had parents that had money. Dandra's mother was a prostitute and only slept with rich men. She'd probably had 80

percent of her classmate's fathers. Life was so hard for her she couldn't win for losing all the times.

The lunch line finally started to move. Dandra picked up a hamburger, some French fries, and a chocolate milkshake then she went to her seat. The 3 divas grabbed their salads, a bottle of water,

and then went to their tables.

"I am so ready for prom this April. I have a few ideas for how I wanna get my hair, what color I want my dress to be and everything" Shantale spoke first.

"If I do decide to attend, I need a fine I mean smoking hot date so we can go to a hotel afterward." Gena said next.

"I thought you had to be an adult to get a hotel room." Shantale said as if she was from Mars.

"Well that's for everybody but me. I am grown and I do what I damn well

please." Gena told her.

"My mom is always down my back. She watches my every move lately." Shantale confessed.

"I turned 18 on January 18th. Therefore I am a grown ass woman. I can do whatever the hell

I wanna do, ok." Gena chuckled.

"Um-mm... sweetie you were grown way before your 18th birthday." Whitley told her friend.

"True that," Gena said giving her a high five.

"Well I won't be 18 until March, but I have been grown ever since I started my period at 12." Whitley said with a smirk on her face.

"Can you guys believe high school is almost over? We have been here for 4 years. It seems like just yesterday we were graduating from 8th grade. Now it's about to be high school. Have y'all started looking at different schools to attend this fall?" Shantale asked.

"I am debating between Howard and Michigan state. They are both really good schools and I can afford both. What about you guys?" Whitley replied.

"It don't matter to me, all I'm gonna do is apply to a bunch of schools and whichever one accepts me that's the one I will go to. My parents can afford the tuition. My grades haven't been that great this year. It's that simple" Gena said.

"Are you serious right now?" Shantale quizzed her friend.

"As a heart attack, college aint really my cup of tea. But to please my parents, I'll go.

And they are paying for everything. Besides college has hundreds of fine men to choose from, crazy parties, and your own dorms. I can't lose with that" Gena explained.

Dandra arrived at the house a little after 4 that afternoon. Her four younger siblings were in front of the TV. They loved to watch cartoons as soon as they walked in from school.

Daisy, her 33-year-old mother walked in the living room wearing a short red leather skirt, a low-cut blouse that showed everything but her nipples. She had on some brand-new red pumps and a bright red lipstick. Her hair was cut low on one side and long on the other like the hip hop group Salt and Pepper. She was a beautiful woman, but growing up she was in and out of foster homes.

At sixteen years old she got pregnant with Dandra and had to become an adult really fast. She did everything from sale drugs to even selling her body just to make money. Sleeping with rich men, which mostly were white men was her favorite job.

All she had to do was get them off and she would leave the room with no less than two hundred bucks. The bills got paid, she could support her five kids, and keep herself up.

"I am on my way to work. Cook them that chicken its thawing out right now. And help the twins with their homework.

Tyshonda and Ambrosia can do their own thing. But be in this house by ten o'clock." Daisy informed her oldest child.

Most teens would fuss back at their parents for making them watch four younger siblings. However, Dandra was used to this and it had been this way since she was eight years old. In a way these were her kids. She cooked, cleaned, helped them with their homework, and did their laundry. All Daisy really had to do was keep shelter over their heads and food in their refrigerators. After kissing her four younger kids,

Daisy rushed out of the front door.

"Dan, I am hungry" Ambrosia her 7-year-old little sister whined.

She was the baby girl. Not only that but she was gorgeous with curly blonde hair and a light complexion to match it. Everyone except for Daisy said that she was mixed. But in reality, Daisy didn't know because she wasn't really sure who the baby's father was either. Dandra wondered if her mother knew who fathered even one of them.

Tyshonda was eleven and very quiet. All she did was read and watch TV. She made excellent grades in school. She was a dark brown complexion but had long hair and the prettiest small hazel eyes. All five of them were great kids. They were really no trouble, but if they did get out of hand, Dandra knew how to get them back in line as well.

"I'm about to cook. Did you have any homework Ambrosia?" Dandra asked her baby sister.

"No, I am only seven we don't do homework yet." Ambrosia replied in the cutest little voice.

Dandra went into the kitchen to see what exactly was in the refrigerator.

As usual the house was a mess and the laundry room had piles of dirty clothes that needed washing right away.

She placed a load into the washing machine and then opened the fridge.

It was a head of lettuce, a pack of chicken thighs, some ground beef, and a bottle of Daisy's brandy.

Dandra put on a pot of rice, she would fry some chicken, boil some rice, make a homemade brown gravy, and English peas for dinner.

She put the clothes into the dryer once the load stopped.

"Darious and Darelle go get your backpacks so I can help you with your homework."

The boys got up and ran to their bedrooms. They were very obedient and always listened to their older sister. She was more than a sister, more like their mother.

After dinner she watched a few hours of TV with the kids.

At 8:30 she gave them their baths. Then she tucked them into their beds. By the time she finally got a chance to sit down, it was

11 o'clock. Dandra took out her homework and stayed up for a hour doing it.

The front door opened at 3 am. Daisy came in looking like she had been at a real nine to five.

"Hey, are they all in the bed?" she asked Dandra.

"Yeah, the boys didn't fall asleep until eleven. Which day are the food stamps coming? We are almost out of food. We have one thing of ground beef left?"

"Tomorrow I gotta go pick em up, I guess y'all can go pick up some groceries when you get out of school then."

"OK"

"What did you cook? I am starving girl."

"I made some fried chicken, rice with a brown gravy sauce and sweet peas."

"OK, go to bed, get you a few hours of sleep."

"Goodnight Ma"

"Night baby"

Dandra could hardly stay awake at the bus stop the following day.

Keri her best friend held her seat when she got on the bus.

The bus was filled with the normal students who lived nearby. Dandra sat down yawning.

"I'm sorry, I didn't get a chance to sleep until like three this morning.

I had to cook for the kids, help them with their homework, put them into the tub,

bathe them, tuck them in, then do my own homework. My body is about to shut down at any minute.

"Well you better wait until after school. Its crunch time and you know you are trying to get into a good school."

"You too"

"I have told you over and over again that college aint for me."

"College isn't for me, isn't Keri." Dandra chuckled.

"Whatever, I'm gonna be making money while you're studying for some hard math exam."

Once the bus arrived at the school, everyone got off and headed to their classes or to the cafeteria for breakfast.

Dandra and Keri went to the vending machine so she could get a drink with some caffeine to keep her woke.

Shantale and Gena were posted in the hallway along with some players from the basketball team.

"Hey Dandra, Tyrone said he wanna take you to prom." Gena teased.

"Hell na'll! I aint said nothing about that ugly ass girl." Tyrone snapped.

Then they all laughed out loud.

Dandra rolled her eyes and took a deep breath.

"Don't even sweat that girl. They some rich spoiled, stupid kids.

And why Gena talking she has been with everybody on the entire team." Keri said loud enough for them to hear her.

"I hate them so much. They have something mean to say about me every day. Sometimes I just wanna kill myself." Dandra said to her friend.

"Don't ever think like that. They are bored with their little simple lives.

For some reason they are very interested in yours. You should feel somewhat honored."

Dandra laughed as Keri walked her down to her class.

Wednesday on the ride home, Keri had some good news for her friend.

A rising pop star named Craig Maddox was coming to town for a concert.

"I got 2 tickets to go see Craig Maddox tonight at the civic center, wanna come with me?"

"Craig Maddox?! I would love to. But I don't have any spending money."

"So what, I got you. So are you gonna come or what?"

"I have to, mama can find a babysitter tonight."

"We are gonna have so much fun!"

"Yeah, we barely get to hang out because of my little brothers and sisters."

"But they probably won't even notice you're gone."

The house was spotless when Dandra and Keri entered that afternoon.

Daisy came in with her purse on her shoulder.

Dandra could already see this wouldn't end too good.

"Ma, can you get a babysitter tonight? Keri invited me to go to a concert and I really wanna go." Dandra said to her mother, almost too afraid to ask.

"Yeah, I don't see why not. Just as long as you got a ticket for your sisters and brothers." Daisy shocked her and said.

Dandra looked at her friend in disbelief.

"But Ma, I am here with them every day, I never get to go out." Dandra explained.

"As long as I am buying the food you eat, the bed you sleep in and house you stay in, you will do what I say. Now I'm going to pick up groceries and get my nails done." Daisy said heading towards the front door.

Dandra flopped down on the sofa and covered her face.

"I'm so sorry Dan. I tried... I'll come back once the concert is over." Keri told her friend.

Keri waved at the kids and left out of the front door.

Dandra sat there and cried her eyes out. What was the purpose of even being alive? Her mother wanted her to be her personal nanny. Then at school all of her peers teased her. Why did she even have to be born?

Daisy stayed gone for hours, Keri had even made it back from the concert before she did. She had a t shirt and a poster in her hands.

"Girl! When I say he is bad, I am talking about Michael Jackson bad. He did all his hits and then a few new songs. And I knew all of them. I had a ball; too bad you couldn't come." Keri told her friend.

"Please don't rub it in, and to make matters worse, she hasn't been back." Dandra informed her friend.

"Really? Dang that was messed up though. Here I know I couldn't bring you to the concert, so I am bringing it to you. I got an autographed poster from Craig just for you."

A huge smile appeared on Dandra's face. This was the nicest thing anyone had ever done for her. She was happy for once.

"That is so sweet of you, thanks girl" she said giving her best friend a hug.

"No problem, it's the least I could do since your mom did what she did to you."

Gena and Shantale went to Whitley's house after the big concert.

The house was gorgeous with 3 levels, 6 bedrooms, 5 full baths, 2 kitchens, a den, her father had an office there, a huge pool, and jacuzzi out back.

Her dad was a very handsome Italian sport's agent. And he only worked for the most famous athletes. Her mother was the head nurse at one of the best hospitals in the state.

She was African American and very beautiful. Twenty years ago she and Edmondo met at a friend's wedding. It had been love at first sight. They dated for only six months before tying the knot.

Then two years later they conceived a gorgeous baby girl, who they named

Whitley. She was their world and she got whatever she wanted. Over the years their careers have gotten in the way of their love life and they finally grew apart.

Yet they remained married for their daughter's sake.

"That Craig can get it anytime, anyplace" Gena said biting her lip as if she could taste him on it.

"He is hot, but he is like 25." Shantale informed her friend.

"And that's the perfect age for me. He is a grown man. Boys our age are so immature and stupid."

"Yeah, you think that now because you've had all of them." Whitley said with a sly grin on her face.

Gena gave her the middle finger.

"Is sex really all you think about, and no thank you?" Whitley said back to her.

"No, it's not... but what's wrong with my sexuality?"

"Gena you are only 18 and you act like you're twenty-eight, we have our whole lives ahead of us. Your mind is just always on boys. Why not be like normal girls and be into fashion, school, and famous men that we know we won't ever have." Shantale informed her friend.

"That all sounds boring as hell."

Time flew by as the girls reminisced on the concert.

Edmondo entered the bedroom a quarter before one a.m.

"Hello ladies, its late you all should be getting to bed.

School will be here in a couple of hours." he informed the girls.

"Ummm... Ma did I tell you about the time I saw daddy's secretary on

her knees in his office?" Whitley said looking dead into her father's eyes.

"Ladies, enjoy your night." he smiled and hurried out of the room.

"Oh my god! If I did that to my dad he would have taken off his belt and beat me right in front of y'all." Shantale said in disbelief.

She couldn't believe Whitley had been so disrespectful to her father.

"OK, my daddy is black, and he would have beat the black off of me if I ever did that to him." Gena agreed with Shantale.

"Please, I have dirt on both of them, that's how I get what I want from both parties."

"Must be nice, where is the phone so I can call my baby?" Gena asked her friend.

The girls left Whitley's house around 2:40 am that night.

Gena went to see her man while Shantale went home to bed.

Her mother was still up when she entered the house.

"Where in the hell have you been at this time of hour?

My mama used to have this saying, don't nothing stay open this late but legs. Have you been out with one of them fast ass boys?!"

Shell snapped at her eldest child.

"You don't care anyways. Go get high and leave me alone. "Shantale caught herself actually saying to her mother.

Shell knew her daughter was telling the truth. Every since their father passed drugs became her husband. It was the only thing that could calm her nerves and keep her happy. Now she was slowly losing her daughters and they were all she had left of him.

CHAPTER 7

A crush

Dandra sat on the porch Saturday afternoon watching the cars pass by. The kids were inside in front of the TV watching their cartoons. Daisy was gone to the mall and Dandra had nothing else to do. It was late February and the weather was fair for a change. She, like most of the town was sick of the twenty and below degrees.

A group of boys headed down the street bouncing a basketball. One of them was Spencer Watson. He was tall, slim, dark, and handsome. He always kept a nice low haircut and dressed in the latest fashions. Since elementary school, Dandra had been dangerously in love with him. In her mind no other guy existed, and Spencer was a nice guy. Unlike the other jerks at school, he never teased her. She wanted him to be her first boyfriend, her first kiss, first lover, and the first man she would have kids for. And even though she knew he was a nice guy, Dandra realized he was out of her league. There was no way he would give her a second look.

Monday, Dandra was in class writing a love letter to Spencer.

Of course she would never be brave enough to give it to him. But the idea alone satisfied her. Gena and Spencer were also in class with her. The only thing the students were required to do was show up and they would pass for the class.

Gena noticed that Dandra was busy writing something and the teacher hadn't given out any assignment. She was very curious to find out what was on the paper.

Then their teacher stood up and headed to the door.

"Class, I am going to make copies of your assignments. Stay in your seats until I come back." Mrs. Gonzalez told her class.

Gena smiled; this would be the perfect time to get the letter from Dandra. She watched closely as

Dandra continued jotting down words so passionately.

"What chu' writing over there Dandra?" Gena asked her classmate, chewing and popping her bubble gum at the same time.

"It's nothing" Dandra softly replied. She knew this wouldn't end too well.

Then out of nowhere Gena stood and snatched the paper off of Dandra's desk and then flopped down in her seat.

She schemed through the note and then she did the unthinkable.

"Sitting in class bored as usual. The only reason why I even like this class is because Spencer is in here. He makes me melt every single time

I look in those big brown eyes of his. I can't help but stare." Gena read the the letter out loud.

The class quickly started laughing and looking at Spencer as if he had caught a fatal disease. Dandra was so embarrassed that she jumped up and ran out of the class in tears.

Why did Gena make it her lifetime goal to make hers a living hell?

Dandra knew she couldn't face the class again, so she decided walk home. $$$$$$

The walk home was even worst. She cried the entire way to the house.

Now Spencer knew the truth. How could she face him now? Of course she knew he didn't like her back, but now the whole school would know it as well.

Today was one of the worst days of her life.

As soon as Dandra entered the house, she rushed into the bathroom and pulled a bottle of pain killers from the medicine cabinet.

The tears were never ending as she wiped her eyes to read the back of the bottle. Just as she was about to open the bottle, Ambrosia came into the bathroom. Her school bus had just dropped her off. She looked up at her sister.

"Dan I gotta use the bathroom." she said walking over to the toilet.

Dandra smiled at her little sister. Her coming into the bathroom was definitely a sign from God to not take her life.

Once all of her siblings were home from school, Dandra went to check the mail. Spencer was walking by bouncing a basketball.

Dandra kept her eyes on the ground. She had been embarrassed enough for one day.

"Aye Dandra, you got a sec?" she heard someone ask her.

She turned around to make sure she hadn't been hearing things.

"What is it?" she answered him dryly.

"I just wanted to say I'm sorry about today in class.

That was real dumb of Gena to do you like that. She aint nothing but a bully, and I didn't think that was funny." Spencer confessed.

"You don't have to apologize for ignorant people.

Either she's lacking attention at home so she's acting out,

or she doesn't have too much self-esteem about herself." Dandra said as if she was a psychologist.

Spencer couldn't help but chuckle at her comment.

"Aye I think you kinda fly though. We should chill tomorrow after School." Spencer surprised her and said.

"But where at?"

"At my house if you down. My grandma works late tomorrow."

"OK, I'll see you then."

"Aight"

He flashed her a sexy smile then walked away. Dandra ran into the house and into her room. She placed a pillow over her face and let out a loud scream. This was one of the worst and best days of her life. She realized she needed to thank Gena in a way. If she hadn't read her note out loud Spencer wouldn't have known she was crazy in love with him, and he wouldn't have asked her to spend a couple of hours after school with him.

Once Dandra got herself together she called her best friend.

Keri had her own phone line, so she answered after the 2nd ring.

"Hello" she said?

"Keri, guess what!" Dandra exclaimed.

"What is it girl?"

"School was horrible. I was bored in Law enforcement, so I wrote a note about Spencer. And then the teacher had to leave to go make some copies. Gena gets up and snatches it from me and reads it out loud. Spencer heard it and everything. I was so embarrassed that I left class and walked home" Dandra explained.

"That bitch... she needs a good ole' fashion ass whooping." Keri cut her friend off.

"No, let me finish. So I went to check the mailbox just a few seconds ago and Spencer walked by. He apologized to me and said he thought I was fly.

And we are gonna hang out tomorrow after school." Dandra proudly informed her friend.

"He did? That's great, I told you not to sweat them! But I do have a question for you."

"What's the question?"

"How are you gonna get there with your mama always asking you to babysit your sisters and brothers?"

"I didn't think about that... I need a plan and fast."

"OK, I got this, just bring some clothes to school and you can come to my

house afterwards. I will do your hair and help you get ready over here and then he can come get you from my house." Keri suggested.

"Great! Let me find an outfit and then I will call you in the morning."

"That sounds like a plan. I am so excited for you!"

"Thanks Keri, you know more than anyone that good things don't usually happen for me."

"Yeah, but your life is about to change. Once we graduate and you get into college all sorts of guys will be after you. And you will finally be away from the 3 bitches from hell."

The friends both laughed out loud at the comment.

The next day Dandra was so excited to wake up. She for the first time had something to look forward to, and that was the opportunity to hang out with Spencer. This was something that she wanted for so long. And to finally have it was almost seemed unreal.

Then she thought about her mother. She would kill her once she decided to come home, but hell Spencer was worth the ass whipping.

After getting her clothes packed, she rushed out of the house.

Keri was smiling once Dandra sat down next to her.

"Ooh let me see what you brought" Keri said as she grabbed the bag from her friend's hands.

Keri frowned once she saw what was inside.

"I know you don't dress that good, but you could have at least found a better outfit. When we get to my house, I will give you one of mines.

You will not embarrass me today."

"I tried to get into my mom's closet, but she was still at home when I woke up."

"I don't know what this is. But I will get you together."

Once they got to school, Spencer met her at the bus lot.

He gave her a hug then they headed into the school.

"So are you ready to hang out with me today?" he asked her.

"Yeah, I'm gonna go to Keri's house after school to change. You can pick me up from there."

"Cool, my grandma won't be home until late. She works late on Tuesdays and Thursdays."

"What are we gonna do?"

"Just talk, watch some videos and chill."

"OK"

At lunch Keri caught up with Dandra.

"So are you excited for the date? When we get to my house I will do your hair and make up for you. I'm excited, I can finally use my cosmetology skills on someone other than my mannequin."

"OK, I need it washed and blow dried too."

"So do you wanna look cute, mature or sexy?"

"Cute will do because I don't want him to think we are gonna have sex because we are not."

"OK, I can find something cute for you to put on."

Once school ended the girls walked to Keri's house. Every now and again Dandra thought about her mom.

She knew she was waiting on her arrival. However Dandra was more excited about her date with Spencer to leave.

The girls went straight up to Keri's room when they got to her house.

"Let me look into my closet to see what I got that you can fit." Keri stated as she rummaged through her closet.

It was about ten minutes later before Keri came up with a perfect outfit.

She pulled out a lime green tank top, a black mini skirt and some lime green ballerina flats with a bow on the tip of the shoes. She washed Dandra's hair and straighten it, then she pulled it up into a high ponytail and a cute bang. She put her on some big gold hoops and some red lipstick.

Keri gave her friend a mirror to check out her make over.

A smile appeared on Dandra's face. She was very impressed with her new look.

"You look amazing" Keri told her.

"I feel it, thank you so much. I didn't think I could look this good."

"Now whatever you do, don't let him get too close to your hair.

It took me a while to get your hair this straight. And please act mature,

don't give in. Make him work for it" Keri informed her friend.

"Trust me, there is no way we are getting busy tonight."

"It's after 4 your man should be on his way over."

"He does know where you live right?"

"Yeah he walks by here all the times with his boys."

"I am so nervous; I have never been around a guy by myself before.

Especially one that I have a crush on."

"Just sit there with your legs crossed. Don't smile, guys love it when we act sexy and quiet. If he does tell some jokes, laugh, but not too hard.

Show him some interest but not too much. Do you get me?"

"I guess" Dandra chuckled.

Then there was a knock at the door.

They looked at each other and then smiled. It was no turning back now.

Keri ran downstairs and slung the door opened.

Spencer stood there in a fitted white t shirt, some black jeans, a pair of Adidas sneakers and a gold wishbone necklace around his neck.

He was too fine for his own good. Keri even noticed it, and if her best friend hadn't been so in love with him, she would have him all to herself.

Dandra came down seconds later. Spencer's mouth dropped as soon as he laid eyes on her. This was not the same girl he attended school with all of these years. This was not the same skinny, quiet, lame girl that everybody teased. This was a pretty, mature, young woman that was hip and had crazy sex appeal.

"You look pretty" he complimented his date.

"Thanks, I did her make-up and outfit." Keri butted in and said.

Dandra turned and gave her an evil stare.

They said their goodbyes then the two headed out. Keri stood in the window smiling and waving as if Dandra was her daughter going out on her first date.

"Dang girl you look good. Why don't you dress like this at school?" Spencer asked.

"Because I don't go to school for fashion or to impress anyone there. And if I was to start dressing like this I would get talked about for trying to look hip, so I rather keep looking the way everybody is used to seeing me." Dandra made a valid point.

"How come when we not at school, you be in the house all the times?"

"My mom works nights and I have to take care of my younger siblings.

So besides school I have no social life." Dandra explained to him.

"Dang that's a lot on yo plate it seems like."

"Ha-ha you have no clue to what it's like."

"Does yo mama ever spend time with them?"

"She has them tonight against her will. But I needed this break. I have them all day every day. I cook for them, I clean for them, I put them to bed, I help do their homework. In a way I am all they know."

"Yo mama lucky all she gotta do is pay the bills."

"She's gonna become a mother really soon whether she knows it or not."

"What do you mean by that?"

"When I graduate, I'm going off to college and I am not coming back here.

So either she will hire a full-time nanny or become their mother full-time."

"So where is yo pops?"

"When you find em, let me know. My mom had me a 16 so he was a kid himself I guess."

"Damn, so what do you like to do when you do get free time?"

"I love to day dream, mostly about my future and how I wish my life could be. That's all that keeps me sane to be honest right now."

"I feel the same way."

"I don't wanna talk about me anymore. Tell me something about you."

"What do you wanna know? It's not like my life that interesting."

"I beg to differ; you always seem so happy. All the girls like you, you have a lot of friends, you're popular. You have no choice but to be a happy person."

"That's at school, I might not have a horrible life. But it aint what it's cracked up to be either."

"How is life outside of school then?"

"I work part time to help my granny pay the bills. I live with her because

my mom died when I was 3 and my pops somewhere strung out on drugs. I really like basketball and I wanna play when I go to college."

"I hope that happens for you."

They finally made it to his house. It was this cute red and brown small brick house.

Spencer unlocked the front door for her and then he let her walk inside first.

The house was decorated with nice paintings, mirrors and pictures of various family members.

Everything was so clean, and nothing was out of place.

It was the complete opposite of her home. There was always a toy on the floor, a few spills on the carpets and crayon marks on the walls.

Dandra always did her best to keep it all clean but she could only do so much.

"Do you want something to drink?" Spencer asked, sticking his head out of the kitchen.

"I'm fine" she smiled.

Moments later he came out with two glasses of soda.

"I know you said you didn't want anything, but I got you some pop just in case you did get thirsty." he informed her.

Dandra smiled as she took a sip of the drink. He was so sweet and knew exactly what needed to be done to make her happy. They sat on the sofa quietly until Spencer decided to say something.

"Do you wanna watch some music videos?"

"Yeah, that would be cool."

"You so shy, but it's OK. You can chill...relax I don't bite."

"I know, you gotta realize this is my first time being around a guy."

"I'm a cool guy so you don't have to be so tense and uptight."

"I really don't know how else to act."

Dandra sat all the way back then she crossed her legs.

She thought back to what her best friend told her earlier. Spencer couldn't help but stare at her long gorgeous legs. They looked so smooth and soft. He could only imagine what it would be like to be in between them. The TV came on after he pressed a button on the remote control. He changed it to the music video channel.

"I wanna dance with somebody" by Whitney Houston was on at the time.

Dandra loved herself some Whitney and she wanted her records so bad, but she couldn't afford them.

"I love every song that she comes out with." Dandra informed her date.

"Yeah she can sing too… as a matter of fact you kinda look like her."

"I wish, she is gorgeous."

"And you look good too."

"Yeah right"

"Yo, you need to work on your insecurities."

"Why?"

"Because you just as pretty, smart, funny, and cool as any of them other females I know at school."

"You would have never known that if you had never taken the time out to hang out with me. Kids at school they take one look at me and think I'm lame. They don't think I'm worth their time so I don't even try to get to know them either. I have one friend and that's all I really need."

"Well you got me too now."

"Thanks"

Watching music videos became boring after a while.

Spencer soon grew an appetite, so he decided to cook for them. He went into the kitchen and put the leftover meat loaf into the oven. He joined her back on the sofa once it was baking.

"I hope you like meatloaf, besides pizza my Granny doesn't let me cook." he told her.

"Well growing up I had to cook or me and my sisters and brothers would have went hungry. And my mom can't even cook that well. I'm really the only cook at home."

"Do you dance?" Spencer asked her out of the blue.

"Yeah, a little bit, why did you ask?"

He got up and turned on the radio. They would dance to pass time until the meatloaf warmed up.

"Rock steady" by the Whispers was playing when he turned on the radio.

At first Dandra just rocked from side to side and snapped her fingers.

Spencer shook his head as if her was her dance instructor.

"You gotta feel the music. Find you a grove and then let your body take control" he insisted.

Before they realized it they were dancing away.

Then all of a sudden there was a smokey aroma coming from the kitchen.

Dandra stopped dead in her tracks.

"Something is burning Spencer." Dandra informed him.

They went into the kitchen and there was smoke everywhere.

Spencer took two oven mittens and took the pan out of the oven.

The meatloaf was burnt and covered in smoke.

Dandra fell over laughing at it. Spencer was not a man for the kitchen.

He smiled as he opened the fridge to see what else there was to eat.

"Oh cool we can make some ham and cheese sandwiches if you cool with that" Spencer told her.

"That's fine with me."

She watched as he took out a loaf of bread, lettuce, mustard, mayo and two slices of cheese. He fixed a pitcher of Kool-Aid and took out a bag of potato chips to go along with their sandwiches.

"When your grandma works like this, what are you usually doing?"

"I go play basketball, do my homework, or chill with my boys if I don't have to go to work of course".

"I'm usually doing laundry, cleaning up, or helping my siblings with their homework assignments. It's kinda weird not having any chores to do right now."

"Do you think yo mama left them home alone tonight?"

"I honestly don't know, I hope not, but I can't worry about that right now.

I am really enjoying myself." She said, flashing him an innocent smile.

"Me too, you are cool people."

After they ate, Spencer took her into his bedroom.

He had posters and a small basketball net hanging on his wall.

"You love Michael Jordan I see" Dandra said looking around the room.

"Yeah he is the greatest player of all time. There will never be another MJ."

"I like Magic Johnson more." Dandra told him.

"He all right, but he aint gon' be no Mike though…

Out of all the dudes at our school, what made you choose me?"

"Well you seem so different from other guys and I think you're kinda fly" Dandra said looking down at the floor. She was so shy and now he had her on the spot.

"That's cool, you pretty fly yourself."

He turned on his radio and "Caught up in the rapture of love" By Anita Baker was on.

"You wanna slow dance?" he asked, reaching for her hand.

Dandra stood and wrapped her arms around his neck.

He smelled so good and his body felt as if they belonged together.

Spencer was getting turned on in the worst way. She was soft and her scent drove him insane. He rubbed her arms up and down.

Then he looked into her eyes.

They stared at each other then slowly their lips moved closer and closer to each other.

He kissed her slowly, pulling her closer to him. Then they fell onto his bed, still Interwind in an lustful kiss. Dandra gripped the back of his head. It tasted so good as he sucked on her tongue, he wanted her more and more with each kiss. Before his hands reached her breast she stopped him.

"We will have plenty of time to get to that point. I should get home before it gets too late" Dandra told him.

"OK"

He helped her get her things together then he walked her down to her house.

They even held hands as they walked. Dandra wished in her mind that this moment would never end.

"I had a lot of fun today with you." she informed him.

"Me too, you are a lot of fun. Aye don't tell nobody about that meatloaf ordeal" he smiled.

Dandra started laughing right away. Just the thought of the smoke and Spencer trying to put the fire out like Smokey the bear tickled her all over again.

"You thought that was really funny didn't you?" he chuckled.

"I did, I see why your grandma limits your cooking."

"Nah, it was really your fault."

"My fault, why do you think it was my fault?"

"The way you had me caught up in your world. It made me forget all about that damn meatloaf."

"I must have that kind of effect on you."

"You do"

They finally walked up to her front door.

"All right, well I better go in before someone comes out and embarrasses me" she joked.

"OK, goodnight"

"Goodnight Spencer"

He grabbed her hand and softly kissed her on the lips once more. Then she watched him walk back towards his house.

Dandra wanted so bad to run after him and never look back.

She knew that once she entered this house, it would be hell to pay. However now was time to face the music. She couldn't turn around now.

CHAPTER 8

Falling for you

Dandra walked into the house feeling like she was on cloud nine.

Being with Spencer was a dream come true. He treated her so good and she loved him with her entire heart.

Daisy came out of the kitchen as soon as she heard the front door close.

"Where in the hell have you been all damn night? You knew damn well your ass was supposed to be here to watch the kids. I had to miss work because your fast ass was out doing who knows what with who knows who!" Daisy snapped.

"I was out with a friend." Dandra simply said.

"Out with a friend, damn a friend! Your brothers and sisters need you here with them! I aint got one day to take off to keep food in y'all mouths or clothes on ya backs. You know to have your ass home every day as soon as school lets out." Daisy added.

"I am here with them every day. They are not even my kids, so I think I deserve to have a day to myself for once."

"Hell no unless you about to pay some bills up in here!

Selfish ass, you know they need you, but you neglect them to be with a friend. Do it again and you gon' be moving where ever your fast ass was at!"

"I can't wait until I go to college. I'm never coming back here.

So you should find you a new nanny or be a mother to your own kids for a change." Dandra heard herself slip and say. It was supposed to be a thought, but it was too late to take it back now.

Daisy slapped her before she realized it.

Dandra gave her mother a hateful stare then she ran to her room. Her perfect day had made a turn for the worst.

She decided to call Spencer once she had calmed down.

"Hello" he answered the phone

"Hey, it's Dandra, do you have a minute?"

"Yeah, what's going on?"

"My mom and I had a big fight just now. I hate her so much. She called me selfish. But I am raising her kids while she goes out and does God knows what with all those men. And I am the selfish one? I can't wait until I go off to college. I am never coming back here. She really thinks in her sick mind that those are my kids and not hers. She even slapped me. Ooh I am soooo done!" Dandra went on holding back the tears.

"Yo mom aint right."

"I know right? I try to be the best daughter I can,

but she doesn't even give me credit for it. I feel like she is using me. Not once has she told me thank you. My childhood was taken from me because I had to grow up fast and raise my sisters and brothers.

These are her damn kids!"

"Calm down, we graduate in a couple of months and you can finally do what you need to do to live yo own life."

"This is going to be a long couple of months. But I did enjoy our day together."

"Me too"

The following day, Keri was anxious to find out how the big night went.

She smiled and scooted over so Dandra could join her on the seat.

"Tell me how your date went." Keri couldn't say fast enough.

"It was great, we watched some music videos, we danced, we made out and then I went home." Dandra said as if it was no big deal. Truth be told she couldn't be happy because her mind was still on her mother. The way she blew up at her for going out one time was wrong.

"That's all? You don't sound like y'all had that much fun."

"I'm sorry girl, we really had an incredible time.

But it was all ruined when I got home."

"Oh shoot yo mama went off on you huh?"

"She did... she slapped me and said I was selfish for not coming home and taking care of the kids. I don't remember going to the hospital to deliver not one of them. She really believes in her sick mind I am their mother and not her."

"No offense, because she is your mom, but she has it all messed up. You are 17 and these are the years where we are suppose to explore, experience life to the fullest. She has no right to keep you from doing that."

"Well guess again because I am just a slave to her. I swear when I go off to college I am not ever coming back. Either she will hire a nanny or become a mother to her own kids."

"What was it like being alone with a boy for the first time?"

"It was really scary, but he was a real gentleman and I felt secure with him. He didn't pressure me to do anything and it was nice. I can't wait until we get a chance to hang out again."

"How with your mama?"

"I will just invite him over once she goes to work one night."

"Cool, was he a good kisser?"

"He was a great kisser; I can still taste his lips on mine."

"Dan is a freak, I knew it." Keri chuckled.

School was all right that day for Dandra. She made it her job to stay low key.

The last thing she wanted was to run into the 3 witches from hell.

However, they couldn't hurt her as bad as her mother had the night before. It was as if her perfect first date with Spencer had never happened.

He caught up with her after lunch. They gave each other a hug.

"Hey, I aint seen you all day." he informed her.

"Yeah, I've been low key today." she replied as they headed to her class.

"Why, what's up?"

"I'm sorry, my mom just really upset me last night.

We aren't best friends, but we never argue. I just always do what she tells me. And when we fought last night I just feel like I will have to defend myself here at school and now at home."

"I don't want you to feel bad. I won't let anybody hurt you if I can help it."

"Thanks, you don't have to do anything special for me. Just keep doing being who you are."

"Hey, I gotta head to lunch, I wrote this letter for you. I'm not a writer so excuse the handwriting, but I hope it cheers you up."

"OK, will I see you after school?"

"Yeah, I'm gonna ride the bus home so we can talk."

"Sounds good"

"See you later"

He kissed her on the cheek before running down the hall.

At that moment Dandra forgot all about her problems. She had the man of her dreams, and they were into each other. Fighting with her mother seemed to have disappeared from her mind after that.

Once in class, Dandra put her books on her desk and opened the letter.

> *Dandra,*
>
> *This has been cool getting to know you these last few days. I gotta admit to you that I had a crush on you as well. But I didn't know how to tell you. I don't care what people have to say about us. They don't know you like I do, and we are good together. You have a beautiful smile, body, and soul. A guy would have to be stupid not to like you.*
>
> *I know we just started hanging out, but I can't deny what I feel inside. I like you a lot and I wanna be your man. If I am moving too fast for you just let me know. But if you feel the same way that I do, let's try to make this work.*
>
> *Love,*
>
> *Spencer your man*

Dandra ran over to her best friend as they got onto the bus.

"He asked me out! He wants us to date!" Dandra exclaimed.

"Spencer?"

"Yeah, he asked me in this letter. My heart hasn't stopped racing yet. He is really my man now. Oh my goodness it happened so fast."

"Did more happen during your date than your telling me?"

"Of course not... it was just that we clicked and he feels the same way that I do."

"Congratulations, this is karma. I do all this and that for these dudes and you don't, and you get a boyfriend before me."

"But guys ask you out all of the times."

"But I don't want them I want a good guy like Spencer. But they don't go to our school."

Spencer got on the bus moments later. Dandra smiled as he sat next to her.

"That letter was really sweet, and I say yes to us being together." Dandra said first.

He leaned over and gave her a kiss on her lips.

"I gotta go to work for like 4 hours. But I'll call you once I get off." he informed her.

"I will miss you, but my sisters and brothers will keep me busy. My mama might just decide to not come home tonight just to teach me a lesson." Dandra joked.

"Oh damn, if she does that, I'll call child services on her my damn self" Spencer chuckled.

"What do you do at your job?"

"Nothing big, I just unload the truck when we get in shipments at the market. I just work there to buy my video games and sneakers. My grandma said I needed some kinda job the way I like to spend money." he smiled.

"She seems like a wise woman; I didn't get the opportunity to meet any of my grandparents and I don't even know if they still exist."

"Why not?"

"My mom grew up in foster care. She doesn't even know if her parents are alive or not. So we just stopped asking her about them."

"Damn, I don't know what I would do without my Granny."

"She's practically your mother. And I really don't have one of those."

Spencer walked Dandra to her house. Then he gave her a hug and walked to his job from there. She watched from the porch as he disappeared down the street. Love was written all over her face.

Daisy was still there when she entered the house.

She looked at her daughter. The night before had been a crazy night for them both.

"Y'all turn that TV off and let me talk to Dan for a minute.

And take them crayons with you. And hurry up, I am not gonna tell you again." Daisy told the 4 younger ones.

They all gathered their toys, and books, and then headed down the hall way.

"I know you hate me right now. I had no right to hit you like that last night and I am so sorry. That will never happen again, I swear to you. You are a good daughter and you haven't brought home any babies here. So I am proud of you and thanks for watching your little sisters and brothers. They are some great kids as well and it's all because of you... here" Daisy said then she handed her daughter something in her hand.

Dandra opened up a 100 dollar- bill.

"What's this for?" Dandra quizzed her mother.

"This is your senior year of high school. This is just a little graduation gift from me. If you ever need a break just let me know and I will hire a babysitter. But let me know ahead of time."

"No, thanks Ma... take this and buy the kids something with it."

"No, this is for you, the kids are doing fine. Just take the money and enjoy it OK?"

"OK"

"Come here, I love you Dan... you were my first baby."

She wrapped her arms around her daughter. Dandra rested her head on her mother's chest. For the first time it felt as if she had a mother and not an older sister. The feeling made Dandra very emotional.

She felt a tear roll down her cheek.

If her mother would have never gave her the hundred dollars and just the apology she would have been just as happy.

After the two made up, Daisy asked her could she leave the kids with her and Dandra was honored to do so. Then her mother smiled and headed off to what she knew as work.

Saturday Spencer had the day off, so he took Dandra out on a real date. They went to the state fair. It was filled with older people, kids, teenagers and couples from all over the state. It felt so good to be out and with her man. Dandra hadn't stopped smiling since they got there.

They got on every ride there. Dandra could barely walk after the last one.

Spencer thought it was so funny to see her trying to catch her breath.

"Aye you wanna get on another ride?" he asked her.

"Uh no, I don't want to look at another ride." She chuckled.

Then this girl walked over to them. She was tall, slim, light brown skinned, and pretty in the face. She was holding a big stuffed animal and had a cute painting on her left cheek.

"Long time no see Spencer." the girl spoke up.

"Hey, how you doing Angela?" he asked her.

"I'm good, you look good too."

"I am, who you here with?"

"Just some friends from school. Graduation is coming up soon."

"Yeah, it is, you made any plans for college yet?"

"Uh... yeah I have a few plans. Nothing is really final though."

Then she looked down at Dandra as if she saw some gross bug on her.

"Oh my bad, Angela this is Dandra Byrd. And Dandra this is Angela my ex-girlfriend." Spencer introduced the two.

"Hi" Angela said dryly

"Hey" Dandra said just as dry

"Well I gotta go, it was good seeing you Spence and you too Dandruff" Angela said walking away.

"Its Dandra, heifer" Dandra snapped.

She was so pissed off that she started walking in front of Spencer as if he wasn't with her.

"Aye wait up... you in a hurry somewhere?" he asked as he grabbed her arm.

"Yeah, I am in a hurry to get the heck away from you" she cried!

"Yo, what's the problem Mama?"

She started walking again as if he hadn't said a word to her.

He ran and stood in front of her so she couldn't leave him.

"Dan what the hell is wrong with you?"

"If you are that stupid to know then I am too stupid to remember."

"Stop the games and just tell me."

"I thought I was your girlfriend, yet you introduced her as your ex and me just as Dandra. Are you really embarrassed of me?"

"I wasn't thinking, I didn't even think it was that big of a deal.

I am sorry you happy now?"

"No! You can't just apologize like that and then think it's ok.

It's not and I am not gonna be with you if you are ashamed of me."

"What the hell am I ashamed about? You been mistreated so damn long that you don't even know how to act when someone does treat you right."

"Why didn't you tell her the truth?"

"I was nervous, I haven't seen her since we broke up and I got caught off guard. If it will make you happy I will go tell her that we are together and everything."

"No, that's OK."

The following day came and Dandra invited Spencer over to hang out. They went into her mother's room. She turned on the stereo and locked the door.

He joined her on the bed.

"Its warm out today, I can't wait until the summer comes" Dandra told him.

"Does that mean you'll be wearing less clothes?" he chuckled

"Yeah when we go to the beach or something."

"What if I want a strip tease from you?"

"Spencer, what kinda girl do you think I am?" she laughed.

"You are a undercover freak aren't you? I will find out watch me."

"What should we do? We can watch some movies, go for a walk, talk, or just sit here."

"When can I show you how much I really like you?"

"What are you talking about Spencer?"

"I mean... we have been hanging out a lot and you know how I feel about you. And I think we should really take this to the next level."

"You mean by having sex?"

"I mean by making love."

"I don't think I am ready for that. But when I am ready I want it to be with you. I just don't think we are ready anytime soon."

"But I want you so bad."

He got up and climbed on top of her. Slowly he started devouring her lips and tongue as if he wanted to swallow them. Then he rubbed her breast up and down in his hands.

Dandra felt herself get moist between her legs. If she didn't stop this boy and fast they would end up all over this bed and floor.

Then his hands went inside of her panties. He rubbed her pearl in a circular motion over and over again as he kissed her lips.

She could only moan and kiss him while he made her flow like a river. When he had had enough of that he pulled down her jeans and pulled her legs apart. Instead of taking off her panties he just moved them to the side. She was beautiful and he had to taste her. He kissed her pearl over and over again then he softly sucked on it. Dandra grabbed his head and gripped it as he kept going on and on. Her knees started to buckle, but that only made him kiss,

suck and lick her harder.

The more he tasted the more of her he wanted. She started screaming and moaning so he put a pillow over her face.

In a matter of moments she exploded in his mouth and he drank her dry.

Dandra could only lay there in silence. What he had done to her had never been done to her ever. It was as if he took her body to an paradise without even leaving the room.

If love making was this good she wouldn't have her virginity for much longer.

He washed his face then joined her on the bed.

"Did you like that?" he asked her.

"A lot… I have never felt like that before."

She put on her clothes and then went into the bathroom and got into the shower. She closed her eyes and replayed the ordeal that just ended. He was so special, and he was always doing something that made her even more crazy about him.

One day she would let him make crazy love to her and they would fall madly in love with each other. The more she got to know him the more she yearned for him. He was her soulmate and she would die feeling the same way.

CHAPTER 9

Graduation blues

The big day had finally come, and the seniors were all ready to say their farewells at
 Downer High. Today was graduation day, after today they would all be considered adults.
 Spencer and Dandra took his grandmother's car to the ceremony.
 "I am so nervous, what if I mess up during my speech?
 There will be hundreds of people looking dead at me today." Dandra told her boyfriend.
 "You won't mess up stop saying that Dan. I am proud of you and so is everybody else. Not too many dudes can say that their girlfriend was their class valedictorian." Spencer bragged.
 A smile appeared on her face. Out of all the honor students in her class she was chosen to be the valedictorian. Today would be a great day for her.
 Once they arrived at the school, they stepped out of the car in their blue and gray gowns.
 Dandra looked at herself in the mirror and applied more lip stick to her full lips. Since this would be her last time seeing all of her loser classmates she decided to dress up. Her mother went all out by

getting her hair did at a salon, her nails done, new shoes and a pretty dress all for her big day. Daisy hadn't made it home yet once Dandra left for the graduation. But she would come and bring her siblings to watch her during one of the most important days of her life. Spencer took her by the hand, and they walked inside of the school.

Keri ran over to them as they entered the gym.

She screamed and hugged Dandra.

"Look at you, my girl is the valedictorian." Keri smiled.

"You look beautiful. I am so excited we are finally done with this hell hole. It seems like it took forever." Dandra replied.

"What are you doing after the ceremony?" Keri asked her friend next.

"I will probably go home and pack. Mom is taking me to see the school this weekend."

"Sounds like fun, I'll probably start at the factory in a couple of weeks until I decide what I'm gonna do with myself."

Dandra knew Keri wasn't an A student, but she had so much potential.

To hear her say she would settle at the city clothing factory made Dandra feel so bad.

So many of their classmates graduated or dropped out of school just to end up there. The pay was horrible, and the hours were even worst. But people did it just for the steady paycheck. Dandra would kill herself before she ever settled like that.

After their talk it was time to go get ready for the big event.

The school band played a slow melody as the class entered and took their seats.

Parents were crying, taking pictures, and cheering on their graduating class.

Then the principal stood behind the podium once the class was seated.

"Good afternoon to you all. We are here to celebrate the high school years of the class of 1987. They were all just babies when they entered the doors for the first time during their freshmen year.

Now they are about to enter into the real world as adults. It was a pleasure to have met each and every one of you. Be wise in every choice you make in life keep God first and never settle. This year the valedictorian is one of our honor students. This young lady has been on the principal's list every semester. She is very shy,

but has a heart of gold. It is my pleasure to announce her as the class of 1987's valedictorian, I give you Ms. Dandra Byrd" Principal Huges said.

People clapped as Dandra made her way to the podium. She hugged her principal then she got ready to do her speech. She looked out at her classmates and their families. There was no turning back now.

She waited for them to settle down before starting her speech.

"Good afternoon everyone. My name is Dandra Byrd. A lot of you all may not even know who I am. I was not one of the popular kids that attended Downer high. But

I am thankful to be standing in front of you as your valedictorian for the class of 1987.

This is the last official day of high school. Most of us never really thought this day would come and I am one of them.

After 13 long years we finally made it.

We are now headed to the real world. High school was a tedious journey for us all in some way, whether if it was getting good grades,

making the football team, dating the cutest boys or being popular.

Here we have learned everything from world history to linear Equations, and what days to skip lunch in the cafeteria. (the audience laughed) After we throw off our hats we will no longer be seniors here at Downer High. We will be young adults in this huge world. There will no longer be the teachers giving extra credit just so we won't fail the course. Our parents will no longer be the alarm clocks that make sure we get to school on time.

We will have to figure out this thing called life on our own.

To my fellow classmates I wish you all the best. I pray that you all explore this big world of ours and make every dream come true. I pray that we set high goals for ourselves and accomplish them all. I pray that we make mistakes and learn from them. And remember that the only one who can determine your destiny is yourself. We did it, God bless you all." Dandra said perfectly in her speech. The entire class stood and gave her a standing ovation.

After saying her goodbyes to her friends and classmates Dandra and Keri went home together. Dandra was still upset at the fact that her mother had bailed out and decided to not even show up at the most important day of her life. How could she miss such a important day?

They entered the empty house. The telephone started ringing before they could walk into Dandra's bedroom. She was in no hurry to answer it either.

"I can't believe she didn't come for real Keri. That was just low of her. No one from my family was even there. If I didn't have Spencer and you I would be a lonely and depressed girl."

"I can't believe your mom was that selfish. I usually don't say much about your mom but that was low. You can miss one day of work for your daughter I mean come on."

Dandra flopped down on her bed and snatched the phone from the cradle.

"Hello" she asked?

"Hey, thank God your home Dan. I really need your help. I didn't mean to miss your graduation. I got arrested this morning and my bail is 250 dollars." Daisy explained to her daughter.

"What?! Ma what did you do? Don't even worry about it I am on my way now."

Dandra hopped off of the bed and ran to her closet.

There was no way she would let her mother stay locked away in jail especially not since she was on her way to college and her siblings needed her the most.

"I swear I am the parent and she is my daughter."

Dandra said as she put on her shoes.

"It does seem that way."

"Well hey I would love to go, but I gotta go get ready for this dinner. And please let me know how it goes. And you are welcomed to come it starts at 6" Keri said heading out of the door.

"OK, I hope I can come if it doesn't take them long to release her.

Spencer should be home by now. I'm gonna walk down to his house and see if he can take me downtown."

"Sounds good, congratulations once again, and I will see you later on."

They gave each other a hug then Keri left out of the door.

Dandra put on a pair of shorts and a t shirt then she walked out of the front door.

She walked down the street to Spencer's house.

During that walk she was able to do some thinking. In less than a few weeks her life would change forever. She would be away from her family and best friend. Her life would be completely different. She would be surrounded by college aged people, she wouldn't have to answer to anyone and she could do whatever she felt like doing.

She would no longer be a mother to her younger siblings. She would get to enjoy her life for once.

Then again she would miss Spencer a lot. He was going to college down south so they would only see each other over the holidays. It would be so hard to see him only every few months. But that was how life turned out for them.

As she got closer to his house, she saw that someone was standing on his porch. The closer she got the better she could see.

To her surprise it was Angela and she did the unthinkable and kissed Spencer on the lips. But what made matters worse was the fact that he didn't even stop her. Dandra felt her heart fall from the ground out of her chest. She turned around and ran home as fast as she could.

After crying her eyes out, she got on the bus and rode downtown to get her mother out of jail.

Shantale drove right home after graduation. The house was almost empty when she walked inside. Her younger sister, Angelica came in behind her. Their mother came in from the kitchen.

Her eyes were huge and red. The girls could tell that she was high.

"How was the graduation?" Shell asked the girls as if she hadn't been invited to the most important ceremony in her daughter's life thus far.

"Where is the sofa and our TV?" Shantale ignored her mother and asked.

"Hmm, that set stopped working so I had a friend get rid of it." Shell said scratching her neck as if she believed her own lie.

Shantale rolled her eyes and went up to her room. She knew her mother was lying so there was no reason to entertain her.

Ever since their father died, the real Shell had died in a way as well.

She no longer knew how to be a parent to her girls. All she knew how to do was get high and stay to herself. The girls practically raised themselves.

Later on that night Shantale came downstairs for a snack.

The telephone rang as she opened the refrigerator.

She hurried and answered the phone.

"Hello" she said with an attitude?"

"Hello, is Ms. Shellie Lorman available?" The Caucasian man asked on the other end of the phone.

"What is this about?" Shantale asked as if she was her mother.

"Hi, Ms. Lorman this is Parker from First Regions bank.

I was calling you about your house. The mortgage hasn't been paid in over 6 months and your home is about to go into foreclosure."

"I'm sorry, did you say 6 months. My husband left me 5 million dollars in that bank."

"Well our records show that you barely have 300 dollars left in this bank. Now we are willing to work with you, I can get you scheduled to speak to a loan counselor and set you up on a payment plan. But if we don't get some kind of payment or the full seven thousand dollars your house is going to be put up for sale."

"Wow... I must say that I had no idea. I will call you in a couple of days thank you."

She put the phone on the hook and stormed up to her mother's bedroom.

Shell was surprised when Shantale slung her door open.

"Girl you scared me." Shell said holding her chest as if she was having a heart attack.

"How come you didn't tell us we were in foreclosure?

The bank just called; you haven't paid our mortgage in over 6 months!

We got like 300 dollars in the bank. What in the hell did you do with that 5 million dollars Daddy left us?!" Shantale yelled at her mother.

"Calm down, I am still your mother whether you like it or not. This house note is 3 grand a month and we have been here for 13 years. You are driving a 30,000-dollar car and I have to feed you and your sister. And your dad was in 2 million dollars' worth of debt before he died. It's by the grace of God we made it this far"

Shell explained.

"That is still not adding up. What the hell are you doing with all that money? I aint stupid I know Daddy left us money and then you sold his things and got more money. If he knew you would do us this way he would have never left you in charge of our money."

Shan confessed. She was getting madder by the seconds.

"You can't tell me a damn thing! You go around here shopping every weekend! Eating out at a expensive restaurant each night and always needing money for school. Yeah I get high once or twice a week. But that's my damn business! So don't you ever storm your ass in my room telling me shit!"

"You liar! You get high every single day and I am sick of it!

You don't have to be a parent for me, but Angelica needs a mother. I am leaving because you are not gonna bring me down. You need to get some help before it's too late."

After the talk, Shantale ran across the hall to her room and started packing. She burst into tears and she loaded her belongings into the trunk of her car.

Angelica came outside to see what was going on.

"Where are you going Shan?" Her baby sister questioned her.

"I'm moving out... I can't stay here anymore with Mom.

We don't see eye to eye, and she needs to grow up and be your mom before it's too late."

"But you are all I have. Who is gonna look out for me when you leave?"

"I will call you every day I promise."

"I love you Shan"

"I love you too"

She gave her sister a hug then she left to find her own path.

After a short drive she decided to go to a burger joint to get a drink. As she stood in line this girl came in the door. She had on a flashy outfit. She wore long colorful nails and her hairs was done up.

It was Vanity Smalls. She had graduated just a few years before Shantale. In school she was much mature than most girls. She dressed like she was going to a club every day and she only dated guys that were out of school. In a way Shantale and her friends envied her.

She was about 5 ft 6 inches tall, had thick thighs, long legs, a nice backside and juicy lips. She was a red bone and most guys would consider her as attractive.

"Shantale is that you?" Vanity asked her.

"Oh hi, what are you doing here?" Shantale replied trying to sound happy

"Girl nothing much, you graduated today right?"

"Yeah I did, what have you been up to since you graduated?"

"I been stripping at club Regal for a couple of months now."

"Stripping? Why?"

The 2 got their drinks and went and sat down at a booth to talk.

"Why not should be the question? After graduation you gon' either end up pregnant and get on welfare, or work at the city factory for pennies a week, or strip and bring home that real money. I make 2oo a night there. And I got my own place, 2 cars, and I can do whatever I want. So if I gotta shake my ass for a while to get ahead, then that's what I'm gonna do." Vanity gave the 411 to her former classmate.

"That does sound good, I don't even know how I'm gonna pay for college."

"Aye let me know, they hire everyday down at Regal.

You better let me know soon at that."

"Sounds good, but I don't know how I feel about getting naked in front of strange men."

"I promise you it's not as bad as you think. All you gotta do is have a couple of drinks, smoke something, and you'll feel like you're on cloud nine."

Spencer got home after his grandmother and uncle treated him to a dinner to celebrate his big day.

His grandmother sat him down once they got to the house.

"I am so proud of you Son. You have graduated from high school and so many of our people couldn't get this far.

Back in my day if you made it to the 9th grade it was just like having a college degree. Times were hard and we couldn't worry about an education. We had to be home and help our families out in the fields. I wanted to go to school so bad. But I knew what was more important at the time. Nowadays education is the only key to having a successful life. I want you to go to college and get a degree then get that good paying job. And I want you to stay focus. Them little ladies are going to be after you, but don't let them distract you from doing what you are suppose to do. Your mother would be very proud of her baby boy. So make us both proud and be all that you can be. Can you do that for your granny" his grandmother explained to him?

"I can do that for you" he smiled.

"That's my boy"

She chuckled as they gave each other a big hug.

Then she gave him a letter that came from one of the schools that he had applied at.

His stomach started doing flips as he opened the letter.

> Dear Spencer,
>
> We are sorry to inform you that you were not accepted into Madison University. We have not been pleased with your G.P.A or we have reached the enrollment limit for the year. Thank you so much for your application. Please feel free to apply again during the next semester.
>
> Thank you once again for your application.
>
> Sincerely,
> Madison University

Spencer balled up the paper and sighed.

"What is it Son?" his grandmother asked searching his eyes.

"I didn't get in after all. They turned me down Nana."

"So, apply somewhere else. Don't you dare let one place stop you from trying. God has the right school for you ready."

"I don't really want to right now."

"You will once you calm down. It's all right to be sad. But you can't stay down. You have to try again."

A few hours passed then the doorbell rang.

Spencer went out on the porch and saw Angela. He was very surprised to see her.

"I just came by to say goodbye" she spoke first.

"Where are you going?" he asked her.

"I am going to the navy. I leave for training on Monday. Then I'll be stationed in California for 6 months."

"Dang, good luck with that."

"What are you gonna do now that you are out of high school?"

"Was going to Madison, but I didn't get accepted. So I don't know what to do now."

"Just apply somewhere else."

"Now you sound like my grandmother."

"Well it's the truth, she is right. Don't let one school cause you to give up."

"Yeah, I guess"

"I will miss you... to be totally honest I never really got over you when we broke up."

"But you broke up with me."

"And I am sorry, I was young, and I thought I was missing out on something else. But in reality I had everything with you."

All of a sudden she leaned in and kissed him on the lips.

At first Spencer just stood there in shock. Then he thought about Dandra and pushed Angela off of him.

"What the hell was that?!" he asked her.

"I'm sorry I guess I got carried away."

"I got a girl now."

"I better go, bye Spencer."

"Bye"

He went into the house and called Dandra. The phone rang and rang. Then he decided to run down to see her. He was surprised to know that no one came to answer his knocks.

Gena walked around the house as family and friends congratulated her on her graduating high school. Her parents had threw her this big graduation party, and so far none of her friends were there. Gena went up to her bedroom and called Whitley.

"Hello" Whitley answered sounding half asleep.

"This is my graduation party where the hell are you?"

Gena snapped.

"Girl my family and I are going through enough as it is. I will call you later on" Whitley said before hanging up the phone.

"That Bitch" Gena said under her breath.

Then she dialed Shantale's number. But to her surprise no one answered the phone.

The party ended a few hours later. Gena's parents decided to have a talk with their little girl.

They all met in the family room.

"We need to talk to you" Tangie told her daughter.

"About what?" Gena asked back.

"You are a grown woman, but we are gonna pay for your dorm room, your books, and your tuition as long as you abide by our rules. There are no excuses, I want you to keep at least a B average.

And if you get pregnant while in school we are washing our hands with you. Be responsible and enjoy your college years. We love you and you know that." Tangie explained.

"If you're not able to handle this much capacity let us know ahead of time and we can cancel this right now." Charles suggested.

"No, I can handle it" Gena spoke up.

Whitley's parents called her into the living room.

The had just arrived home from the graduation. She was so excited it was time for them to unload her with money and her new B.W.M that she wanted since last Christmas.

"We are very proud of you for getting this far in life.

I remember bringing you home from the hospital. Now you are my young lady. But in my mind you will always be my little girl. We want you to take life and ride the hell out of it." Edmondo said to her.

"You have always been so head strong, and I don't ever want you to change who you are Whit. Your father and I love you so much and we only want what's best for you. That's why we waited this long to tell you that we are getting a divorce." Patrice confessed.

"What did you just say?" Whitley asked her mother.

"We are getting a divorce Whitley. You have your way of manipulating us to get what you want, and I am tired of it. Your mother knows I cheat, and she isn't happy with me. Now that we have raised you we can stop the lies and move on. It's over now" Edmondo explained.

"Is this a corny graduation prank or something?" Whitley asked as she searched her parents eyes.

However they didn't look as if they were joking in the least.

"Honey, we have kept these charades going for years for you. Now that you have stepped into the adult world, we can move on and be happy." Patrice said next.

"I am so sorry; I only wanted a new car. But it's OK I can take a Honda or something. Please don't do this because of me.

I need the both of you. I was so stupid to blackmail the both of you, but I will never ever do it again. I will give back the money, the jewelry, clothes and shoes" Whitley begged.

"Honey this was not your fault. Your father and I have been planning this for a while now. This has nothing to do with you. Our terms as a married couple are over. We waited until you graduated high school so you should be happy to know you didn't grow up in a broken home." Patrice informed her daughter.

"Thanks for the best graduation gift ever." Whitley said then she ran out of the house.

She got into her car and burst into tears while driving out of the drive way. At that moment she had no clue to where she was going. But she did know that she was going to go as far away as she could from her parents.

After 20 minutes, she ended up at the town's lake.

Whitley wiped her eyes and turned off the car. Then she got out and walked down to the edge of the water. She sat there and watched the fish swim back and forth. At that moment she didn't care about her clothes, her hair, or her make up. So much was on her brain. How could her parents do something so cruel to her?

Who would she go home to during school breaks? Who would come support her at school functions? Then reality kicked in, Whitley knew this was all her fault. All she ever did was take from her parents and blackmail them. They gave her the best life they possibly could,

but that was still not enough for her. Now she would be split between the two of them. It was not supposed to be this way.

"Are you ok?" a male's voice asked her.

She looked up to see a familiar face.

"Spencer, what are you doing here?" she questioned him wiping her eyes.

"Whitley?"

"Yeah, it's me" she said holding her head down.

He sat next to her on the ground.

"What are you doing here, all alone? And have you been crying?" He asked her.

"My life was supposed to begin today, but instead its ending.

I found out my parents are divorcing" Whitley confessed, trying so hard to

hold back the tears.

"Dang, that's messed up. I am sorry to hear that. But hey you aint alone. I didn't get into Madison, then Dandra has been avoiding me all day long. So this aint a good day for either one of us." Spencer informed his friend.

The 2 ended up talking for over an hour. He even made her laugh a few times.

"You are really cool Spencer. Dandra is really lucky to have you." Whitley told him.

"I haven't heard from her all day. I don't know man... love is crazy" he replied.

"You really love her?"

"I do, she is an amazing person and I wish I could've known this before senior year."

"That's really sweet, she seems so happy now."

"She doesn't have the three musketeers tormenting her anymore." Spencer laughed Whitley playfully hit her friend on the arm.

CHAPTER 10

I need love

The following day was a Saturday. Dandra had failed to hear from Spencer. Was he guilty and knew that she knew about the kiss with his ex? Or was he just busy getting ready for school just as she was?

Daisy was now out of jail and she promised to stop prostituting. She had a long talk with Dandra. She apologized and paid her back every penny that she had used to bail her out. She told Dandra to go to college and enjoy her life and she was very proud of her.

Keri came over to take Dandra out on the town.

Dandra wore a very beautiful blue dress, a gold belt around the waist, and some blue pumps. Her hair was curled and her full lips were red. She had it going on.

"Girl you look like a movie star." Keri complimented her girl.

"Well thank you so much. I feel like it. Now that I am single again, I gotta look like I am on the market." Dandra smiled.

"So you haven't heard from Spencer?"

"I haven't, but that was high school. I am going to leave him behind.

We wouldn't last if we were a couple being so far away from each other anyways. It's kind of good we ended this way."

"Well good for you. Let's go get our party on."

Whitley got home around 6 that evening. She took a 20-minute shower and then crawled into bed. As she thought about her parents and her life, she couldn't help but cry all over again.

Why couldn't this be a horrible nightmare that she could wake up from? She closed her eyes and tried to sleep but she couldn't.

She decided to lay in bed for the rest of the day.

The following day, Whitley woke up still in a stank mood. She decided to sneak into her father's bandy just to ease the pain. The idea of her parents being separated was still a hard pillow to swallow. As she opened the cabinet, the telephone rang. She walked over and answered the phone. To her surprise it was Gena.

"Since you are home now, get your ass up and ready.

You, me, and Shantale are going to go out." Gena said on the other end of the phone.

Instead of getting into an argument with her friend Whitley went upstairs and got dressed.

Her friends arrived a hour later. Whitley got in the passenger's seat, Gena was driving and Shantale sat in the back.

"I need love" by LL Cool J was playing.

The girls were all going through something in their own lives.

They all started rapping along to the song.

"When I am alone in my room sometimes I stare at the wall and in the back of my mind I hear my conscience call telling me I need a girl who's as sweet as a dove for the first time in my life,

I see I need love" they all sang together.

They went to get a milkshake first. As they sat at their booth, Gena started the conversation.

"I am so ready for college, there will be no parents,

no bedtimes, endless parties, and did I mention the college boys? This is every woman's dream." She said with hearts in her eyes.

"I have to find out how I am gonna pay for school." Shantale blurted out.

"What you mean?" Gena asked her.

"I found out that we are broke, and our house is in foreclosure." Shantale finished.

"Damn, how is that possible? I thought your dad left like so many millions for you and your sister," Gena said.

"He did, my damn mother is an addict, she used up the money on drugs. Our house is empty because she sold all of our things. I feel so bad for having to leave Angelica behind with her. I am scared that she might try to sale her." Shantale replied holding back the tears.

"I am so sorry if you want I can ask my parents to loan you the money."

"No, thanks Gena, but I will find a way to go to school."

"Whit why are you extra quiet?" Gena asked her other friend.

"I am fine, are you guys done here? If so let's go somewhere else." Whitley said finally.

The girls finally got up and left for the theater.

They decided to go see Eddie Murphy's new movie, Beverly Hills Cop 2.

Gena handed her girls their tickets as they walked into the theater.

"Let's go check our make-up. I know it's going to be a lot of fine guys here to see this." Gena said smiling.

"How are they gonna see us if the lights are off?" Shantale asked.

Gena just shook her head and led her girls into the restroom.

Once in the room, they all stood by the sinks and checked out their faces in the mirror.

"OK, truth moment... Whit you have been acting very strange the entire time
 since we got here. What is really going on?" Gena asked her.

"Yeah, you are really quiet" Shantale added.

"Is it obvious? Oh God I hate myself soooo much!" Whitley said covering her face.

"Whit, we are your girls just tell us what it is." Shantale informed her friend.

"OK, you both have to swear that you won't say a word to anyone.

My parents are divorcing, and I got mad and went to the lake. Spencer was there and he and I talked, and we ended up having sex." Whitley confessed.

"Spencer? Dandra's Spencer," Shantale quizzed?

"Yeah, I feel like dying. I lost my virginity to him.

It was incredible, but I can't forgive myself for doing it." Whitley added.

"Wow, this hardly happens to me, but I am speechless off of that one." Gena said.

"It is ok, we all make mistakes. Now let's go see Eddie's fine self." Shantale said to make her friend feel better.

"Shan is right, you aint did nothing to be ashamed of.

We will finish this after the movie, come on. I will get the popcorn" Gena smiled.

She led her girls out of the restroom.

Keri walked out of the stall of the bathroom. She heard it all and couldn't believe it. Then Dandra came out of her stall.

Her face was covered in tears.

"I am so sorry Dan; I had no idea." Keri said wrapping her arms around her friend.

CHAPTER 11

A reality check

Now it's back to the year 2002. The girls all looked over at Whitley.

Not one of them had a dry eye. Hearing how horrible they had been to Dandra brought a tear to all of their eyes. They had no clue how bad they had damaged her.

"I am so sorry. I was really cruel to you." Whitley said over her tears.

"So was I, damn… I am sorry Dandra." Gena admitted.

"Me too, we were all wrong, can you find it in your heart to forgive us?" Shantale asked as humbled as she could.

"Yeah, I guess... I just wanted y'all to realize I have feelings. I am human too. My last year of high school was hell because of you three." Dandra spoke.

"And if we could take it back we would. I can't say I'm sorry enough." Whitley said to her still crying.

"It's only fair to keep my end of the deal. I gotta let you all go now that you have apologized to me." Dandra confessed.

"Thank you Jesus," Gena said closing her eyes.

"You can shower and get dressed then I will have my driver take you home personally."

They all gave her a hug and apologized once more before leaving. Once on their way home, Gena sighed.

"Can you believe we were gone for over a year kidnapped like that?" Gena said to her friends.

"Yes, we are lucky she didn't kill us. We ruined her life.

And it must have really damaged her for her to take this action on us after all of these years." Whitley explained to the other 2

ladies.

"I agree, the bible says whatsoever a man soweth that shall he also reap" Shantale added.

"So where to now? She turned all of our families away from us?" Gena asked.

"I am going to see my father. I feel like I need to apologize to him for being such a spoiled brat." Whitley said to them.

"I know where I have to go first as well." Gena confessed.

With that being said it became clear to Shantale as well where she would go.

They were all ready to face their lives and make the best out of it.

Whitley followed the maid into the family room where her father sat. He had a glass of Vodka in one hand and a remote in the other. He almost froze when he saw his beautiful one and only daughter.

"Whitley my dear where have you been?" he stood asking her.

They gave each other a big hug.

"I was away clearing my head. Papa I came to talk to you. And to apologize for being so evil to you. I am so sorry and I have blamed myself all of these years for the divorce. 2 years ago I had an affair and Kyle left me. He took the kids and he hates me. Why am I such a malicious person? I wanna be humble, understanding, and permissive" Whitley revealed to her father.

He took a deep breath first.

"Whitley, my dear no one is perfect. We all do wrong and it's a part of being a human. But you have choices so stop feeling sorry for yourself. Take responsibilities for your own actions and realize you are not the reason why your mother and I divorced." Edmondo said to her.

She took a tissue from the box and wiped her eyes.

"We fell out of love with each other. We stayed together that long just for you. Let the past be the past. Just live in the present and make better goals for your future. If you don't listen to anything else I say listen to that."

"Is it that easy Papa? I have done so much wrong in my life. I want the pain and guilt to go away. I want to start over.

I am not a good friend; I wasn't a good mother or wife" she started to cry.

"It's not too late to change it. This is your life and you can change it if you are not pleased with it."

"Thank you Papa, I love you so much." she said hugging him as if she would never let go.

Next on her list was Kyle, then her children. She called him from the hotel.

"Kyle Mowry's office, how may I assist your call this Afternoon?" Kyle's secretary answered the phone.

"Hello, I am Whitley Mowry, I need to speak to Mr.

Mowry right away. And please don't tell him that it's me." Whitley informed the secretary.

"Hello, Mrs. Mowry I will transfer you right away."

"Thank you"

"Kyle speaking" he answered the phone in his deep baritone voice.

"Hi, Kyle… it's Whitley" she said feeling like her heart would jump out of her chest.

"Whitley? Is it really you?" he asked as if he was in disbelief.

"Yes, I am back in town. I was wondering could we meet for lunch and talk about some things."

"OK, I'll take my lunch at 2. Let's meet at Jefferson Cafe around say, 2:15?"

"That is fine with me. I will see you then." Whitley said before ending the call.

Kyle stared at the phone once it was back on the hook.

So many emotions were running through him. Did his wife really just call him out of the blue just now? Where had she been for the last two years?

He had to become mother and father to their kids. They all figured she had died after a year. But now he knew that nightmare was all over.

The kids would be ecstatic, but he needed answers. Why did she leave the way she did and not let him know? There were nights that he hired a babysitter just to take long drives in search for her.

The pain still hurt him so badly. He had been the best husband that a man could be. On a daily basis he saw the tape replay over and over again in his head.

And When did he stop being enough for her?

He honestly thought they had the perfect marriage.

She showed no signs of cheating. Their sex lives were already dull because they both worked hard. He would buy her expensive gifts just because, he often tried to surprise her at work with flowers. What woman wouldn't love a man like that?

Whitley went shopping and bought a fabulous dress for lunch and a pair of pumps and pocketbook to match. Even though she cheated and broke up her family, a small part of her wanted Kyle to see her and want her back.

After hours of preparing herself for the date, Whitley finally left the hotel to meet with Kyle.

He was already there when she arrived. He stood once she got to the table. A smile appeared on her face. She gave him a hug and then sat across from him. She was flawless as ever and he couldn't deny her of that.

"You look good" she informed him.

"Thanks, so do you" he replied.

"I want to start off by saying thank you for meeting me today. "

"It was out of the blue to finally hear from you."

"I want you to know that I wasn't running away from you or my kids.

I had to have a reality check and I needed to be alone.

I didn't come here to pour out lies to you or make you feel sorry for me. I am aware of my mistakes and I have lived with the consequences since." Whitley explained.

"Why didn't you call or write? Your kids and I even started to think you were dead. You have missed 2 whole years of your kid's lives and they needed you." Kyle told her.

"And I needed them, you left me. I had no idea where you were and where you took them. After that I decided that I needed to leave and better myself. Trust me you don't have to punish me, I have been doing a hell of a job doing that to myself already."

"I am not trying to punish you for anything. That's something you are going to have to take up with God."

A waiter came over and took their order. Kyle waited for him to disappear before picking the conversation back up.

"Are you back for good now or what?"

"I am... Kyle I want to say that I am sorry for the whole affair. It was nothing that you didn't do for me as a husband.

I was just used to having my way and I wanted my cake and to eat it too. And like I have told you before I am paying for my sins. If you hate me I don't blame you. I just want to be here for my kids and be the best mother I can possibly be to them."

"I think that would be a good idea."

They talked more over a bowl of home style lasagna then Kyle ended the date to get back to work. Whitley watched him leave out of the cafe. Reality had hit at that moment; he was no longer a part of her life.

Gena's first stop was at Cameron's grave. She was holding so much hurt and love for a man who was no longer a part of the living. She needed closure so that she could give her heart to the next man that came into her life.

She sat a single red rose on the top of this tombstone.

"I haven't been out here since your funeral. Of course I had plans to visit, but you try doing something like that with 3 kids. Speaking of kids, Camrey is so beautiful and she looks so much like you. I love her with an unconditional love because she was our child. We actually were making love when I got pregnant with her. My sons are my heart as well, but I was never in love with their fathers. You were my first and really my only love. I can't even move on because in the back of my mind I feel like you are gonna come back to me. It sounds stupid, well not to my heart. You taught me how to be free, how to love, and my own parents didn't even tell me how to do that. Why did you have to go? Thank you for being my best friend, my lover, and my everything all in one. I will never ever forget you.

Save me a seat in heaven. I will visit more and even bring Camrey here to see you. You would be very proud of her. I love you, rest in peace, goodbye Cameron." Gena said before breaking down in tears.

She blew a kiss at the tombstone and then she left.

This was so hard to do, but at the end of the day it had to be done in order for her to move on.

Her next stop was at her parent's ranch.

She rang the doorbell and waited for someone to open the door.

Tangie came to the door moments later. When she realized that the visitor was her long-lost daughter, she froze.

"Hey mama" Gena said to break the silence.

"Gena, oh my God... we thought you were dead." Tangie said with her hands over her mouth. Then she wrapped her arms around her daughter and wept as if she had rose from the grave.

Then she called for Gena's father to come see what the surprise was all about.

He came to the door and froze as well.

"Gena, baby girl we thought you were gone." he said taking her hand and then he hugged her as well.

Then Tangie took her by the hand and they entered the house.

They ended up in the living room.

"Where have you been for over a year?" Tangie asked.

"I had a nervous breakdown, and since I had no one to turn to I left town.

You may not know it, but I was dealing with a lot…

My parents disowned me for having a baby in college. I have three kids with three different men. I have been working two minimum wage jobs just to get by. These jobs don't pay shit without the proper education. Their daddies don't do shit for them. So I have been dealing with all this mess all by myself. Excuse me for my language,

but I am really going through it. And I am here to say I am sorry. I was a fast ass, had to get my sex drive from someone right? But I should have been more careful. But I will never regret having my daughter. And you don't have to speak to me again. But I hated you both for years.

When I needed you the most you turned your backs on me. I am human, I make mistakes. If my daughter came home with twins I would never do her the way you did me… I am done here. I am doing this new thing called getting it off my chest. And now that I have done that here, I can leave." Gena said standing to her feet.

"Gena wait… your father and I have something we wanna say to you too." Tangie informed her child.

So Gena sat back down on the sofa and crossed her legs.

"We are not saying we for one moment are pleased with you for disobeying us, and doing exactly what we told you not to do. But, you are our only child and we did the worst thing that a parent could ever do to their child. I will never forgive myself for turning my back on you. And yes I always carried that guilt around. Baby you were still a baby and the news broke my heart. I felt like you were trying your best to do the opposite of what we told you to do. I am sorry, I am, and I love you. If you can just let me make it up to you I will do that for the rest of my life." Tangie said as the tears poured down her face.

"Your mother is right we have missed out on so much.

And I can't change the past, but we can do all we can to make sure your present and future are better. I love you Gena; you are my only child." Charles added.

Gena was in tears as well. Throughout her life she tried to cry hardly ever. But now she had all these emotions built up inside of her and it was time to release them.

And then she had to find out where her kids were.

"Thanks, I really needed to hear that. It makes me feel so much better to know that. But I have to go now. I have been away for over a year and I have to find my kids. And I will die if I don't find them fast. I didn't intend on leaving them behind, but at that time I couldn't bring them along with me. I will give you guys a call later on, but I gotta go." Gena said standing up once again.

This time Tangie stood up as well.

"Gena before you leave, I think I should tell you something else." Tangie came out and said.

"What is it Ma?"

"We know exactly where your kids are. A year ago when we got the call that you were missing your father and I did what we had to do and got custody of the kids." Tangie confessed.

Shantale knocked on the door once more. Then seconds later Angelica opened the door. She had a weird look on her face.

"Shan where have you been?!" Angelica exclaimed.

"Hey, can we talk?"

"Sure, let's sit on the swing"

They sat on the white swing on the porch.

"I have been calling, stalking Toris, and going all over the place looking for you." Angelica informed her sister.

"I am all right, I had to go away for a while. Toris left me when he found out about my past. So I have been trying my best to deal with that." Shantale came clean.

"Oh no, how did he find out, you finally came clean?"

"It was a Sunday and it was after church. A guy walked over to us and thanked Toris so much for the service. He kept staring me up and down. Then he said he knew me from somewhere. I told him no and he kept at it until he figured me out."

"How did Toris know he was telling the truth? You should have denied it until the end."

"I was until he asked did I have a tattoo on my thigh." Shantale replied.

"Damn, there was no way out of that one." Angelica said being honest.

"Yeah he wouldn't even talk to me once we got home.

He told me to get out of his house and that was that."

"Have you tried talking to him yet?"

"And say what? That I am sorry for lying to you for the last ten years and our entire relationship was built on a lie.

God I hate mama I will never forgive her for what she did to us. If she had saved our money I wouldn't have to strip to pay for school."

"Right that is the best thing to do. Blame Mom, she was the worst mother ever. She made you walk up to that strip club with a gun up to your head, and made you take your clothes off for all of those strange men." Angelica said being sarcastic.

"Angelica?"

"You are so wrong, true our mom was not the best. But she had a lot on her plate. She had to raise two girls on her own. So what she got high and sold our shit, she is still our mother. And we have to love her for who she is." Angelica dropped some wisdom on her older sister.

"She was never there for me. She paid more attention to that crack pipe than she did to us. And I am gonna blame her because she wasted our money on drugs. Now I am lonely and away from my husband because of it."

"No offense, but you really need some therapy."

"And why do I need to see a therapist?"

"Because you are holding in a lot of hate towards Ma and you two need to get to the root of it and build a relationship."

"There is nothing she can say to me. I am done with her."

"You are going to become a bitter lonely woman. If you never listen to anything else I say do this for me. Go see her and talk. You and Toris will not work until you and Ma get a understanding, if you want I will even go with you."

"No, I hate to say this, but you are right. I am at the point that
I will do anything to get my man back."

"That's my girl I will be here for you."

"I'm going to see mom for a while."

"Good, let me know how it goes."

Shell decided to go to rehab 5 years ago after almost overdosing. It scared her straight and after that she never took a pipe or even a pain killer. Shantale had to admit how proud of her mother she was. Now she had to make peace with her so that she could love and be there for Toris. It was time to stop blaming everyone else but herself for her own problems.

Shell was very surprised to see her oldest daughter arrive at her condo. She gave her mother a kiss on the cheek.

"This is a surprise," Shell said lighting her cigarette.

"What does that supposed to mean Ma?" Shantale asked her mother.

"You don't ever come by and see me. I know I am not yo favorite person in the world. But I still love you and you still my baby whether you like it or not." Shell said to her.

"Ma, please can you stop doing that?"

"Stop doing what Shan?"

"Stop acting like everything is okay between us. We have been going at it since I was in the 9th grade. I am here to get closure Ma. I have held hate in my heart for you since I was 18 years old."

"You have been going at me like I am your child or something.
I thought I was your mother, not the other way around.
Tell me what did I do so bad to you?"

"You were never there for me or Angelica. We had to raise ourselves.

You never spent time with us. We had to do everything on our own and we needed a mother."

"I was in no condition to raise a kid. I had my own problems.

Yeah I sucked at parenting, but I can admit it. So if that's why you hate me oh well. We all make mistakes, I will deal with this for the rest of my life."

"See you are acting like it's no big deal! You spent up all of our money that Daddy left us. I had to strip to pay for college. Do you know how degrading it was to get naked in front of strange men? Then some men wanted oral sex, a one-night stand, or offer me drugs to ease the pain. And then I met the man of my dreams.

He was a man of God so I couldn't tell him that I stripped on the side. So I lied so we could be together. But 10 years passed and he found out. Now I am alone, and I have lost everything."

"And it's all my fault? Shit happens all right?

Get used to the real world.... I was in love with your father. He was my air, my breath, my heart, and my soul. We would sometimes think the same thing and even say it out loud at the same time. I would get butterflies every time he walked into the room and this was after we had kids. (sighs) When I got the call that your father was killed, a part of me died as well. I needed something to cope with his death so I turned to drugs. It made me feel so good but every damn time I thought about it, my high would come down. I know I should have been a better parent but drugs were the only thing that kept me from killing myself. "Shell said as the tears built up in the corner of her eyes.

"Ma, I am soooo sorry. I didn't know that you were suffering this way." Shantale as she walked over and wrapped her arms around her mother.

They cried as they held each other. It was the breakthrough they both needed the whole time.

"Toris left me, he found out about my past. And I miss him so much."

"You need to go to that man and make it right. Let him know that you love him, and you will never do anything to question his love for you." Shell informed her.

"I will, and Ma I am so sorry. I will never treat you that way again."

"I forgive you, just go get your man."

"I love you" Shan said kissing her mother on the cheek.

She got into the car and called Angelica.

"How did it go?" was her first question.

"We had a break through. I was so wrong to hate her. She was suffering after Daddy passed. And now that I am married I understand. How would I be if something happened to Toris?"

"I am so glad you did that. The only thing left to do is to talk to Toris."

"I'm gonna call him and see what happens."

Shantale was able to stay with Angelica and her family a while.

Angelica made a delicious meal that night. Shan decided to help with the dishes. Angelica was putting the leftovers into some storage food containers.

"That was really good. When did you learn how to cook like that?" Shan asked her sister as she placed the dishes into the dishwasher.

"Well, when you went off to college I had to cook for myself. It was one of those things you either had to learn or you didn't eat."

"I wanted to take you with me so bad, but I couldn't have you around the environment I was in at that time."

"I often thought about you too and prayed that wherever you were you were safe."

"Thanks, I love you so much. And thanks for letting me crash here until I get myself together."

"Anytime, when are you gonna call Toris?"

"I don't know, maybe tonight. I have never been so nervous about anything in my life."

"Just get it out of the way."

That evening after her bath she decided it was time to make that big call. She sighed as she dialed the digits on the dial pad. Since it was after 3 she knew he would be home. The phone rang several times. Then there was a light silence. That meant someone had finally answered the call.

"Hello," a woman's voice asked?

CHAPTER 12

The summer after

Dandra sat numbly in the passenger's seat that night as Keri drove them home from the movies. It had been a nightmare for them both.

Whitley had slept with her man. She had been angry with him for letting his ex-girlfriend kiss him on the lips. But this was just the icing on the cake. He was actually getting his grove on with one of her worst enemies. She would have been more accepting if it had been with Angela. But to have sex with Whitley, there was no way she could forgive him.

Keri felt the need to finally speak up and console her best friend.

"Dan, I am really sorry about tonight. If I knew they were gonna be there we would have went somewhere else. You didn't deserve to find that out the way you did." Keri said.

"Don't even worry about it. I don't even wanna bring it up again.

If we can, let's act as though it never happened. I'm gonna go home, pack, and leave for school earlier. I am done with that jerk Spencer.

He was a jackass and I will never forgive him. I am hurt, but thank God I didn't have sex with him." Dandra went off.

"True that, them bitches act like they have to have everything, even shit that doesn't belong to them."

"I swear on my life that bitch and her two friends will pay for the hell they have put me through. It may not be tomorrow or next month, maybe not even this year, but I promise you they are gonna pay for this shit."

"Calm down Dan, you are scaring me."

Dandra changed into some shorts and a tank top once she got home that night. Instead of going to bed she did some more packing. The sooner she got out of that house, that city, and that environment the better off she would be. She kept seeing Spencer on top of Whitley stroking her deep and hard. He was her man, and he lied to her. He said he would never cheat or give her a reason to doubt him.

The bastard gave her 2 all in one day. Saying she hated him sounded too nice at that point.

Then there was a knock at her door. Daisy walked in holding the telephone.

"It's for you" she told her.

"Who is it?" Dandra asked loud enough for the caller to hear her.

"It's that Spencer guy I think." Daisy said as if she was half asleep.

"I don't know a Spencer and whoever it is tell them to drop dead."

Then Dandra walked over to her closet, showing her mother she meant business.

"Hello, yeah she said drop dead... OK, bye" Daisy said before ending the call.

She closed the bedroom door and went back to her room.

Dandra flopped down on her bed and grabbed a pillow. Why was her life so horrible? She tried her best to be nice and get along with everyone, yet it didn't help. From that point on she made a vowel to put herself first no matter who she hurt. There would never be another person to walk over her.

Spencer angrily slung open the front door. It was 6 in the evening and his grandmother was gone to work. He was home filling out another college application when someone started banging crazy on the door.

"Keri, what the heck is wrong with you?! You don't come over somebody house knocking like you lost yo mind." Spencer snapped at her!

The next thing he knew was she had slapped his left jaw numb.

"Did you just hit me?" he asked her.

"I did, and I am very tempted to do it again! How dare you cheat on my girl twice in one night! You are a dog and I am glad she dumped your no-good ass. I thought you had so much class and you were different. But you aint no different from any of these other fools out here. How could you, she loved you?" Keri yelled.

"It was a mistake and I only cheated once. Angela kissed me and I pulled her away. But with Whitley she asked me to make her feel better."

"So if she told you to jump off a cliff are you gonna do that too?"

"Can you please leave? I know what I did was bad. And if Dandra never wants to speak to me again I understand."

"Well honestly you are giving yourself too much credit than I'd like. You knew how much she loved you and for you to say she deserves to be mad is an insult. I feel like you did it on purpose. If you only went out with her because she had a crush on you that was really low Spencer."

"I am not that shallow, I really liked her... I actually love her."

"You can stop telling those lies, my girl will get over you and for her sake just leave her alone."

Keri rolled her eyes at him as she walked down the steps and headed home.

The following weekend came, and Dandra was on her way to school. She was going to stay on campus and find a summer job so she could have money for her school clothes and books.

She was packing up the last of her luggage when someone ran down the street yelling her name. She looked up from the car to see Spencer. Dandra sighed as she closed the door and headed back to the house. He ran even faster until he was close enough to reach her.

"Babe, please don't do this to me. Can I talk to you before you leave?" he begged her.

Dandra didn't bother saying a word to him. She politely pulled her arm away from him and headed into the house.

"Dan, Baby say something to me. Please don't shut me out anymore.

I know I messed up. But it was a mistake. I don't want Angela, and I damn sure don't want Whitley. None of them are you."

Spencer went on to say.

"Dan, are you all loaded up?" Daisy asked her daughter.

"Yes, ma'am, I gotta get my camera so we can take pictures when we first get there." Dandra smiled and said to her mother.

She didn't want Spencer to think that because she hated him that she was unhappy. After all the tears and praying she was very much at peace now.

Dandra went into her room to get the camera.

Spencer stood there as if he had no intentions on leaving until they talked.

"Son, I barely know you. But you seem like an decent enough young man.

Dan is my daughter and no matter what she does I will always have her back. Please leave she is not going to talk to you right now. Let her calm down and then when she is ready she will talk." Daisy told Spencer.

"Can you tell her that I am sorry, and I really love her so much." Spencer said.

He had a tear rolled down his left cheek. His eyes were red. She could see that he was really sincere in his apology.

"OK"

Dandra came into the living room moments later.

"Your friend finally left. Whatever he did to you, he is sorry and he really loves you." Daisy told her daughter.

"I don't care how he feels. I'm ready to go now."

"OK, well let's head out. Did you say goodbye to your brothers and sisters?"

"Yes, I can't believe it's finally happening."

"I am so proud of you. Let's get you to your new world."

Daisy kissed her on the cheek and walked her little girl out to the cab.

Shantale walked inside the strip club with Vanity late Saturday night. They were both dressed like they were auditioning for Playboy or something.

Nervous would be an understatement to describe how Shantale felt at that moment.

It was so degrading to see the selection of men looking at her as if she was a piece of meat.

Most of the men looked old enough to be her father, or uncle.

The day before Vanity had brought Shantale down to audition for the owner. After a few moves, he hired her. Today was her first day on the job. She was wearing a black thong and bra with silver little hearts on it along with the 5-inch open toe high heels. She put the s-e-x in sexy.

A guy smacked Vanity on the ass when she walked past him.

Shantale stopped in her tracks because she knew Vanity would go off on the guy. Instead she smiled and winked at him. Shantale knew she would never be that calm if a man disrespected her that way.

Once in the dressing room Vanity introduced her to the other ladies. Some were friendly and said hello to Shantale. Then there were the stuck-up broads who felt threatened and didn't say a word to her.

"I am about to throw up. I am that nervous." Shantale informed her friend.

"Calm down, all you gotta do is drink a couple of shots, and pop one of these and relax. All you gone do is dance real sexy for these niggas and get paid. I promise you it's easier than it looks."

"I sure hope so, let me get that pill and a drink."

"I got ya"

Shantale sat there on the bench once she took the pill.

Finally she felt herself get numb and this intense high feeling. She started laughing out loud. Vanity walked over to her.

"What the hell is wrong with you?" she asked already knowing the answer.

"I feel so damn good. I am ready to go get this money."

"That's my girl, come on we about to go get paid."

Vanity took her by the hand, and they went upstairs to the club. The building was packed. Vanity found a table of 4 men. She smiled at them.

"Would you fine men like a show that you'll never forget?" She asked the guy.

"That's why we're here." One spoke up.

Vanity pulled Shantale close to her and started rubbing her thighs up and down then she started dancing on Shan as if she was her man. The men started throwing money at them.

Shantale walked over to one of the men and started dancing on his lap. He grabbed her breast and rubbed them in his hands as she grind slowly making his nature rise. Surprisingly, she liked it just as much as he did.

The following day, Shantale woke up at 1 pm. She had an terrible headache. It felt as if her head was going to explode. Then she looked over to see some strange man lying there asleep next to her. She snatched the cover off of him and ran down the hall.

She opened the door and Vanity was also asleep with a strange man.

Since she was a light sleeper, she woke up when Shan whispered her name.

She sat up in bed and looked over at her.

"What's wrong girl?" Vanity asked her.

"Where are we and who is that strange man in my bed?" Shantale quizzed her.

"We spent the night here. They the same niggas from the club." Vanity said getting up to get dressed.

"I don't like that idea. Was I that high because I don't remember anything from last night?"

"Girl you got loose; I didn't know you had it in you."

"Was I that bad?"

"If only I could have put it on a camera. But we made over 300 dollars last night alone. So it paid off."

"My money is going straight on school. Can we go home? I am tired and we gotta head back there again tonight."

"OK, get your clothes and we can leave."

Shantale went back into the bedroom where she woke up and looked around for her clothes. They were nowhere to be found.

She cursed under her breath and then went all over the house in search of her clothes. Then she noticed the back door was still opened.

She walked out and saw that her bra and panty was in the hot tub. Instead of taking them out, she decided to just go home in the sheet. It would be more clothing than the bathing suit. Vanity was already in the car waiting on her when she walked outside.

She got in with her and they left.

"Where are your damn clothes?" Vanity asked her.

"I don't know, I can't find them. I really don't like the fact that

I lost myself and woke up with a strange man like that" Shantale said to her.

"Its apart of the job. Niggas are gonna be asking for sex, you to go home with them, do private parties but they pay real good. Now if you can't handle all of that then maybe this aint the job for you."

"That don't mean I gotta freak every guy that comes my way.

And I asked to strip that is degrading enough for me."

"Damn, you make me feel like a whore."

"I didn't say anything about you. It's your life and your decisions whatever you do. But you don't have to drag me along with everything you get into."

"You aint gotta do the shit, I just figured that since we kick it now you would want to."

"No, I don't... and the only reason why I decided to strip is because I needed money for school. If my drug headed mother hadn't smoked up all of our money I would have been be all right."

"You had no other option and I helped you out. If you don't wanna hang out, that's cool. But don't sit up here like I am making you do anything."

"I never said that. All I am saying is after we leave the club I am going home from now on. I don't need to be doing anything else that's gonna hurt my work ethic or anything like that."

"I hear you, but once you see my money is three times larger than yours then you gone start asking me to go do these side jobs."

"I will be all right with the money I make at the club."

Gena couldn't wait until they arrived at the school.

Her parents had talked her head off the entire drive there.

They kept telling her that she would now be on her own, she had to act like an adult and make wise choices. She had to keep a B average in all of her classes. She had to stay away from boys, parties and focus only on her grades. That was the only reason for sending her there.

It was just the beginning of the summer and her parents thought it was a good Idea if they took her down to visit her college for the weekend.

They finally arrived at the school a couple of hours later.

Gena opened the car door and got out of the car. She could hardly believe her eyes. The scenery was breath taking. The campus was huge.

It looked like a mini county compared to her high school.

"This school is huge, oh my God, come on Mama and Daddy let's go look around." Gena said as if she was a kid in a candy store.

"Hold your horses, we are coming. I have to get the map,

and your mother's camera. You know this lady can't go to the market without taking pictures of it." Charles teased his wife before planting a I'm sorry kiss on her cheek.

Once he had everything the trio headed towards the campus. Gena had so many ideas run inside of her head. Once her parents ditched her; she would go on the prowl in search for some late night fun. There would be thousands of sexy, young, horny college brothers to choose from. And she would make sure she didn't stop until she had enough. The campus was amazing and so many great African Americans had went there to get their education. Charles decided to show them the black history hall. It had autobiographies and pictures of different famous African Americans that once taught or were enrolled there.

"And there are many more that will make history and also attend this same school." Charles informed his family.

Gena shyly looked around to see if any cute guys were around her. Then she thought about her late-night plan, it would be her parent's bedtime very soon. She smiled on the inside.

After the touring the school, Charles drove them to the hotel.

"I need a room, 2 beds please" he told the clerk.

"Excuse me, what's the other bed for?" Gena quickly asked her father.

"It's for you Gena" he told her.

"Ma, is he serious? I don't even share my bedroom at home with anybody. So why is daddy making me share a room with y'all?

I don't wanna be in the same room with y'all." Gena complained.

"Come on Charles the girl is right. Why are you even trying to make her share a room with us?" Tangie asked her husband.

"Because we are a family, she can share a room with us for one night."

"I am not going to make her share with us and if she does share the room, were you planning to sleep the entire night?" Tangie said to him, throwing an hint.

"All right, Ma'am, I am sorry make that two rooms.

And yes they do need to be side by side" Charles said handing the clerk his credit card.

Gena smiled as she flopped down on the bed. She had a plan in motion. All she needed was for her parents to fall asleep and then it would be on. There was a knock on the door. Then Tangie walked in to the room.

"Hey sweetie, just came in to make sure you have everything you need for tonight."

"I'm good Mama" Gena said flipping through the channels with the remote.

"Well goodnight, get some rest we are heading out bright and early in the morning."

Once Tangie closed the door, Gena ran over to her suitcase.

She pulled out her outfit and ran into the bathroom. Thirty minutes

passed and she came out of the bathroom in a pair of short shorts, a halter top and some open toe sandals. Then she peeked outside of her room. There was not one person in sight. She smiled and walked out of the room and headed towards the elevator. Once she made it down to the lobby, she walked out of the hotel, and down the busy street.

There were only a few cars on the roads. Gena walked until she spotted what seemed to be a bar. She smiled and decided to walk inside it. Once she was in, she realized it was more like a sport's bar. There were a few white people drinking beers, eating wings and yelling at the TV screens. Then she spotted them. There was a table of these handsome black guys. They must have belonged to some sports team because of the varsity jackets they each had on. It was at least 5 guys and Gena knew one of them was going home with her.

Well to her hotel room at least.

She walked past them, sure that one of them would notice her. And sure enough a few of them started making little comments when she walked by.

Before she could get to the bar, someone started whistling at her. She turned to see this tall handsome caramel colored man.

Gena tried not to lick her lips in front of him. Truth be told she wanted to lick him and then put him up for later. He had it going on with those sexy big eyes, full lips and thick eye lashes.

This guy was definitely a playboy. But Gena was okay with that. All she wanted was some wild sex before heading home.

"You came here alone?" he asked her.

"I did, why?" she replied.

"You aint scared that some crazy guy could grab you up and take advantage of you?"

"Well it may work; I am crazy too." she smiled.

"I like you already, what's your name pretty lady?"

"I am Gena, you are?"

"I'm Phillip and those guys are my teammates. We play varsity basketball for Garrett Tech" he said to her.

"Oh really, I will be a freshmen there this fall."

"Fresh meat... cool. But what if I wanted to see you before this fall?"

"Maybe we can arrange that."

"Where you staying tonight?"

"I have my own hotel room."

"Aye give me yo room number and I can come see you once I leave here."

Once she gave him the room number, Gena gave her new friend a hug and then she left to prepare for her hot date.

While looking at herself in the blue and white laced panty and bra set there was a knock at the door. Gena walked over to the door, and opened it half naked. Phillip's mouth drop he knew she was fine, but damn.

This girl had ass, breast and thighs. She was only 18 in age, but she had the body of an twenty-five-year-old easily.

"Come in" she said then she walked back over to the bed.

He closed the door and followed her like a lost puppy.

There was no reason to talk, after seeing all of this he needed to be inside of her and that was that. Gena crossed her legs and looked into his eyes.

"What do you wanna do?" she asked him.

"Shh I rather just show you."

He leaned over and started rubbing her breast in his hands as he kissed her neck. He twirled his tongue around her chest and then he undid her bra. Gena got under the covers and pulled off her panties. He put on a condom then he climbed on top of her. He kissed between her legs and then slid inside of her.

"Damn it feels like heaven inside of you." he moaned.

"Go deeper.... ooh give it to me" Gena said as she wrapped her legs around his waist.

They went at it for maybe ten minutes then he rolled off of her.

Even though it was fast, they were both pretty satisfied. A smiled appeared on Gena's face as she rolled over on her side.

Maybe college life was all of that after all.

There was a knock on the door hours later. Gena looked at the alarm clock beside her. It wasn't even 6 am yet. Who and why was there someone at her door? She got up and went to the door. It was her mother and she was fully dressed.

"Mama, why are you up so early?" Gena asked trying not to yell at her mother.

"It is time to get up and we are heading down for breakfast at 6. And we are heading home at 7. So go get dressed and meet us down at the lobby." Tangie informed her.

"Why do we gotta leave so early though?"

"Your father has other plans today, plus I do have an hair appointment at 2 this afternoon."

"I'll be down in ten."

Gena sighed as she closed the door and went back into her room. To her surprise Phillip was nowhere to be found. She looked to see if maybe he left a note or something. But there was no sign of him or a goodbye letter. Gena felt bad, that meant she would have to wait until school started to see Phillip. She took her shower and got dressed. Then she packed her suitcase and then took the elevator down to the first floor. Tangie and Charles were both standing there waiting on her. Charles took her luggage out to the car and then the three of them headed to the free breakfast buffet.

After hearing the news about her parents, Whitley went into a deep depression. She stopped eating, hanging out with her friends, or leaving the house. She waited for her parents to leave then she would sneak into her father's cigarettes and smoke 2 a day.

They were the only things that seemed to calm her down.

Finally it was time for Edmondo to sit down and have a serious talk with her. He entered her room the night he got home from a business trip from Rome Italy. He sat at the edge of her bed.

"Are you still sad Bella?" he asked.

"I don't really feel like talking to you or anyone right now." Whitely said as she hugged her favorite stuffed white cat.

"Bella, I will always love you. And I will always be here for you. But you have to realize that your mother and I really tried to make our marriage work. We went to counseling, we prayed about it and everything. But the love wasn't there anymore. And I will still love and take care of you. We waited this long until we broke up. And I have my own apartment now. You are welcome to come stay anytime you want. I really hope you can one day forgive us for making this decision."

"I will never forgive you or Mom for this. I hope you the best at your new apartment and I hope Mama all the best too. But I am not ever coming to see you or her. When I leave for school that will be the end of it."

"I don't understand?! You hated us and you tried to destroy us every time you didn't get what you wanted. And now that we are finally being honest with you and ourselves you can't handle it. Tell me why is it that you can't handle it?"

"I was young and stupid! I didn't think you guys would really split? I told you if it's because of all the money you spend spoiling me, then you can stop. I just want my parents together."

"We tried Bella; we really did. But it didn't work. God we waited 18 long years before it happened."

"I don't even care anymore. All I know is if I get married and my marriage doesn't last, I will blame you and Mommy."

She gave him an evil stare then she left out of the room.

Edmondo was so hurt to know that his baby girl blamed him for his failed marriage. He decided to leave out of the room as well.

Whitley went to the store to pick up a pack of cigarettes.

She was old enough to buy her own pack, so she decided to get them. Plus she hated sneaking around to get one out of her father's study.

While walking to the register, Whitley saw an old friend. It was Spencer, and after their little rendezvous, she had no intentions on ever speaking to him again.

But she had to be a big girl and be cordial. He flashed her a shy grin.

"How you doing Whitley?"

"I'm making it," she simply said.

"You haven't left for school yet?"

"I am waiting until it starts this September."

"Yeah, I'll probably go to a community college and then work my way to a university. Dandra and I broke up."

"I didn't mean to cause y'all to break up. It seems like I am doing that a lot lately. I have to go, and I really think we should stay far apart from each other."

"I thought we were cool."

"I just think we have caused enough drama and we will be miles away from each other so it best that we stay that way."

"Fine, be like that"

She gave the man the 3 dollars for the cigarettes then she walked out of the store.

Once she arrived home, there was yet another surprise waiting for her. There was a huge moving truck there.

Her father came out behind a few of the movers. He was really moving out. Whitley sat in her car and watched as the men walked in and out of their 3-story mansion. Slowly she felt the tears run down her face. When would this nightmare finally be over? Ever since graduation day her life had become this horrible reality. Why couldn't things just go back to the way they were? She wanted her family back. Even though she blamed Edmondo for the entire thing, she knew her mother was a part of this cruel ordeal as well. The both of them needed to sit down and take some counseling. Yeah that sounded great, she would tell them right away.

Whitley got out of the car and headed over to her father.

"Papa, can you and I, along with Mommy talk?" she asked in the sweetest voice.

"Talk about what?" he asked, not so sure he cared what it was about?

"Just come with me please."

The 2 of them walked into the mansion and found Petrice.

"I think you guys should seek some professional help before you Divorce." Whitley informed her parents.

"Sweetheart we have tried all of that don't you think?

There is nothing left in this marriage. Your father and I love you so much. But you are going to have to get over this. We are finished being together." Patrice explained to her child.

"You don't have to make it sound like I disgust you or something like that." Edmondo said to his future ex-wife.

"I'm not, but she does need to know that we are done."

"I give up, I am so done with the both of you." Whitley said then she ran upstairs to her room.

"Whitley, baby wait" Patrice yelled after her.

"She hates us" Edmondo spoke up.

"I didn't think she would take it so hard."

"Me either, but she is young. She will understand it one day."

"I just want to protect her and make sure no man ever hurts her."

"Are you saying I hurt you?"

"Let's not forget that you cheated first."

"I only cheated because you stopped caring for me.

You stopped having time for me. And then you turned around and cheated on me. So you are not the victim here the only victim here is our little girl."

"She is a young lady, most girls her age didn't even grow up with their parents. So she should be thankful she had the both of us this long. Your movers are waiting on you."

Patrice went upstairs to her bedroom. She heard the silent tears come from her daughter's bedroom. She wished there was something she could do to cheer her up or make her understand why this was happening. Instead she went into her room and watched as her husband directed the movers on what to take out of their once happy home.

CHAPTER 13

College Days

Shantale woke up ten minutes late. She ran into the bathroom and got into the shower. She had only 20 minutes to get dressed, drive to the campus, and get to class on time.

This was not the way to start her first day of school.

She hopped out of the shower and then put on some jeans and a designer t shirt. The apartment was a mess when she walked down the hallway. There was an empty wine bottle on the coffee table, a pair of underwear on the sofa and empty Chinese boxes all over the floor.

The night before had been a blast. She and Vanity invited these fine brothers from the club back to their place. They did everything from give

them private dances to even a foursome.

Shantale knew this was not the life style she should have been living, but she knew she was young and had plenty of time to grow up.

Vanity walked in wearing a black silk robe. She smiled at her friend.

"You headed to class?" she quizzed her.

"Yeah, I am, have you seen my history book?" Shantale said looking under the sofa.

"No, are you about to leave me here with them?"

"Yeah, I need my book!"

Then Vanity saw the book on the counter top.

She threw it at her best friend.

"Thanks, I gotta go, I will be back later on."

They hugged each other then Shan ran out of the house.

She finished doing her make-up on the drive to school.

This was her first day of college she was nervous beyond measures.

How would she concentrate on school work, then have to go to work at the strip club every night? She didn't know the answer at the moment, but she knew she would have to figure it out, and very soon.

Shantale hurried to the second level of the building, and after a few minutes of looking she found her class. The students were coming in like a flood. She found a seat in the middle and opened her bag to get out her book and notepad.

It was after 4 when Shantale returned home from school.

Her body was worn out. She flopped down on the sofa next to Vanity who was smoking a joint.

"Here, you look like you need a hit." Vanity said holding the weed in her friend's face.

"No, I don't need no drugs. I have to do a report already.

And I have to read 5 chapters in one of my classes. This college stuff is super hard" Shantale explained to Vanity.

"That's why I wouldn't even waste my time going to school.

I make as much money as a college graduate. I don't know why you even going to college."

"I want to, and I don't wanna strip forever. Plus you can't be a forty year stripper."

"What you trying to say that I'll be a stripper at 40?"

"You act like you will."

"If I do that's my damn business. Don't diss it, hell for now its yo job too."

"Only for a while and when it becomes too much, I'll just quit and get a student loan or something."

"Are you coming with me to the club tonight or what?"

"I have to, but I am leaving after I do my solo. I need to come home and read this book and start on that report. What time are we leaving tonight?"

"11 the same time we leave every night."

Shantale stood up and gathered her things then she went to her bedroom.

Vanity turned around in the mirror to take a look at herself from behind. She smiled at what the results were. Her ass looked juicy and plump in the new black leather dress she was wearing with the black lip stick to match and some crazy black boots. She did a seductive dance in the mirror and then she put her a pair of long silver earrings. The only thing left to do was get Shan and they would leave for the club. She walked into her room to see her asleep at her desk with a book under her face and a pen in her hand.

She walked over to her and shook her. Shan woke up and looked up at Vanity.

"What time is it?" Shan sat up wiping the drool from the corner of her mouth.

"It is almost time to go. You better go jump in the tub and come on."

You aint even started your assignment yet Shan."

"I'm tired! I have been up since seven this morning, and now I gotta go to this club until 4 or 5 in the morning. Then I gotta come back here, sleep for like two hours and then do it all over again.

I am not super woman; I can't go tonight."

"What? You know he aint gon' have that" Vanity warned her friend.

"I will come tomorrow, I swear. But right now my body is not used to all of this. Tell him I got like a cold or something."

"Okay, but this is the first and last time I cover for you."

"Thanks, I'm gonna take a shower and then go to bed."

Gena looked around the room once more. It didn't seem big enough for two grown women. But this was the college life and she would have to make it work. Then the door opened and shut. This pretty chick walked in. She had this long hair; her skin was smooth and mocha colored. She had a nice small frame and her outfit was very stylish.

She gave Gena a radiant smile.

"You must be my roommate, my name is Paula, and you are?"

"I'm Gena, you must have a rich family?" Gena asked right away.

She saw how stylish this girl was and she had the most expensive things. Her luggage was even made by one of the most famous Italian designers In the world.

"Yeah, I was adopted by an older rich white couple.

They couldn't have kids, so they adopted me and some other white girl.

She's a few years younger than I am." Paula told her.

"Interesting, so are you a freshmen too?"

"Yeah, I am... this is a popular college. I always wanted to go here when I was a kid. It's funny how dreams can come true if you believe them long and hard enough. Tell me about yourself Gena."

"There aint much to tell really. This is my first year also.

My parents got money too and since I wasn't a honor student they are paying out of pocket for my tuition. So I have to do well here."

"Oh, I'm sure if you study, pay attention in class and do all of your assignments you will do awesome here."

"Do you have a boyfriend Paula?"

"I did back home. But we are at 2 different schools right now so we broke up. What about you?"

"I sort of had this fling with the guy name Phillip,

he goes here too. But it was during the summer, so I don't even know if he remembers me now."

"I'm sure he does, I'll help you find him if you want."

"You would really help me out?"

"Yeah, I know we are roommates and we just met, but I hope we become good friends as well."

Gena walked onto campus looking finer than a bottle of wine. She had on a low-cut blouse and a cute tennis skirt. This was her first day of school and she was looking for her future man,

Phillip. They had such a good time that night and she couldn't get him off of her mind ever since. Guys smiled and looked her up and down as she walked past them.

Then this woman walked over to her. She smiled once she realized that it was her roommate and new friend Paula.

"Hey girl, what are you up to?" Gena asked her.

"I just left my morning yoga class. I feel so refreshed, you should join me one day. It's a great class to relieve stress."

"I will, I don't have a class until after 1. Do you wanna go grab some food in the Cafeteria?" Gena invited Paula.

"Sure, the food here is awesome I've heard."

The girls said nothing else and headed to the school's cafeteria.

Gena had attended the best high school in the state, but her college made her high school look like a daycare. The

cafeteria alone looked like a mini mall. Paula got in line behind Gena. There was at least 20 different choices for lunch. They had everything from supreme pizza to shrimp fried rice. Gena grabbed a plate of orange chicken and brown rice with a spring roll. Paula on the other hand got a plan salad and a bottle of water.

After long searching they found a spot at the end of a table in the middle of the cafeteria.

"Damn, I didn't realize how huge this place was. I mean the cafeteria alone is like a mall" Gena said.

"Yeah, it's pretty huge, how was high school for you Gena?"

"It was all right; my girls and I ran the whole school.

We used to do everything together. But after we graduated they changed on me like that (snaps her fingers). It's funny how you can spend years with somebody and still not know who they are." Gena explained.

She really missed her girls and thought they would always be friends. But they proved that they no longer wanted that after graduation.

"Maybe they were really never your friends in the first place if they treated you that way."

"I know, but one of my girl's parents decided to split up the day of graduation. And then one of my girls got stressed out when she found out her family was broke, and she didn't know how she would go to college. So I understand how they feel, but they didn't have to shut me out like that."

"True that, back home I didn't have too many friends myself. Girls hated the fact that I was rich, black and adopted by a white couple. So I spent most of my time at home studying for school.

And that's why I'm here now and most of them are at home with kids."

After lunch, the girls threw away their trash and headed back to their dorm room.

To her surprise Gena spotted Phillip hanging with a group of guys. She stopped and smiled. Paula looked at her.

"You are blushing, what is it?"

"That's him"

"Him who?"

"Phillip, the guy that I met over the summer here.

Oh God he looks even more sexier now than he did then." Gena said almost drooling at the mouth.

"Oh, he is fine"

"I want him so bad, should I go say hi?"

"You aren't too scared to go over there alone?"

"No, I am never afraid to go after something I want."

"Okay, I will stand here and wait for you to come back."

Gena switched her hips back and forth as she walked over to the group of men.

Right away the guys started staring at her.

"Hey, Phillip, it's been a while since we last seen each other how you been" She asked him?

"I'm all right, do I know you Ms. Lady?"

"Yeah, we met this summer at that bar downtown."

"Oh, what's up with you?" he smiled as if it all came back to him all at once.

"I told you I would be coming here this fall. When can I see you again?" She boldly inquired in front of his boys.

"Aye when is yo last class?"

"It ends at 6:15 tonight" she informed him.

"Meet me by the cafeteria and I'll get at you."

"Aight, later" she smiled

The guys could not wait to quiz their friend about this hot chick.

"Damn! She got stupid ass on her. Who was that Phil?" Martin asked his friend.

"That was some hoe I met over the summer. She was checking out the campus and she invited me to her hotel room. She let me get the panties the same night." He bragged to his boys.

"It looks like to me she trying to give em to you again." Dale his other friend spoke up.

"So what" Phillip said as if he was no longer interested.

"It don't sound like you want that? Did she burn you or some shit?" Martin asked next.

"Man hell no. I used a condom, but that girl a hoe. She probably give it to everybody that walk pass."

"I thought them was the ones we liked, my bad" Martin teased.

"I know right" Dale laughed

"Aye let me have some and I'll find out if it's worth a second round or not" Dale said.

"She don't seem like the selfish type; you should ask her yourself." Phillip insisted.

"I can't believe you really went over there!" Paula said trying not to get too excited.

"I told you I always get what I want."

"So what did he say?"

"He wants to meet me by the cafeteria tonight after my last class."

"Sounds good, I am so excited for you."

"Maybe he can hook you up with one of his friends."

"No, thanks even though there are some really cute guys here, I need to really study and be successful here."

"Have it your way"

Gena could barely keep calm during class that evening.

She knew that after class ended she and Phillip would go to her room and engage in some long, hot, sweaty sex. She closed her eyes and started day dreaming about him. He would stroke her deeply leaving her body sore with satisfaction. It was feeling so good that she could almost taste him. Class ended at 6:15 on the dot. Gena was one of the first out of the classroom. She rushed over to the cafeteria to wait on her date.

She looked down at her watch and saw that it was 25 minutes after 6.

Maybe he was just leaving out of his class. She would wait for ten more minutes.

Paula entered the room a little after 7. She was suddenly startled, Gena was there sitting on her bed, and it appeared she was studying.

"Hey, I wasn't expecting to see you back here this early" Paula said to her.

"Yeah his stupid ass stood me up."

"Really?"

"Yeah I waited over thirty minutes on him. He never even had the intentions on showing up. Just wait until I see that Bastard."

"He is a real jerk; he didn't deserve you anyways."

"They never do" Gena sadly had to admit.

Gena did her homework assignment for class. Then she and Paula went out for a few hours.

After a while she was happy she had spent her night doing something way more productive than having sex with Phillip.

A few days passed and Gena had yet to see Phillip. While coming out of the cafeteria this guy approached her. He was tall, slim and not that cute. But he was popular and a star on the varsity basketball team.

"You know you gon' have to quit teasing me in these little ass dresses and tight shirts you be wearing" he said to her.

"Excuse you, close your damn eyes then."

"Nah, I rather you open them legs and give me some of that like you doing for everybody else around here" the guy surprised her and said.

"What did you say to me?"

"You heard me Bitch, my boy Phillip said you the go to girl."

Gena felt her heart drop down to her feet. Not only had this MF stood her up, but he was going around telling every dude on campus that she was a hoe. Oh it was on now.

"Oh, is that what he is saying about me?"

"Yeah, so you gon' let me get some or what?"

"Kill yourself" Gena said then she walked away.

She made up her mind to find Mr. Phillip even if it took her all night long.

After 3 long hours she found him in the gym shooting around with some friends.

The ball rolled over to her, so she picked it up, and walked over to them on the court.

"Can you just give us the ball hoe?!" one of his playmates shouted out.

She threw the ball and hit Phillip in the arm.

"Damn, why you throwing shit" he exclaimed?!

"I heard you was going around campus talking shit about me!" Gena shouted.

"Man what you talking about?"

" Don't play with me you dumb ass punk! Would your friends like to know how small your shit was or how you nut in less than 5 minutes Mr. minute man? Huh, should I keep going?"

"Damn! She put all your shit out there." Dale laughed out loud.

"Aye, you better take your ass out of here. That shit is all a lie." Phillip said.

"Do I need to get some more proof? See I found a couple dozen females who can also attest to your short package and weak stamina" Gena told him.

"Get the hell out of here" Phillip told her.

"It will be my pleasure to little man. Let my name roll off your mouth again and see what happens to you. You fellas have a good game."

Gena mean mugged Phillip then she left out of the gym.

Once the word got around campus that Gena had blasted out Phillip in front of the entire gymnasium, she got props from all sorts of women and even guys. Turns out Phillip was a dog and thought he was God's gift to women.

He had hurt so many women.

Paula invited Gena to a big party thrown by one of the seniors.

The party was a house party of course. Gena and Paula made sure to be late so that all eyes would be on them when they arrived.

Gena said hello to some of her classmates. She was becoming more popular by the hours.

"If I could have you Gena, you wouldn't be out here looking for a man." Ricardo informed her.

He was this gorgeous Hispanic guy from Puerto Rico. He loved himself some black women, Gena in particular. She was highly attracted to him as well, but she knew there was no way he would be able to keep up with her.

"Papi, you and I both know that I am too much woman for you." she replied to him.

"That's all in your head Mami." he smiled.

"And what do you mean by I'm out here looking for a man?"

"Come on, I'm not stupid, you are. Every time a guy walks pass you; you stare at him."

"That don't mean I'm looking for a man."

"Come on and give me a chance."

"I don't really think so, maybe later."

"You are afraid that I might sweep you off of your feet."

"If that's what you think, but I will catch up with you later.
 I gotta mingle with some more people."

"Suit yourself"

Gena walked away on a mission to find a guy to dance with and sweep her off of her feet.

The party seemed lame, there was hardly any one dancing and the music sucked.

Gena decided to find Paula and head home.

She was walking up the stairs when this guy bumped into her.

She looked at him with a stare of evil. Then her eyes soften when she saw how beautiful he was.

"I'm sorry, I was in a hurry" he informed her.

"No, I should have watched where I was going" Gena said.

"Sorry again… are you enjoying the party?"

"I wasn't at first, is this your party?"

"Yeah kind of, my boys and I live here, and this is our little back to school bash. But everybody acting all funny. I'm thinking about shutting it down."

"If you do I won't be mad."

"That's what I get for letting a boy do a man's job. This was supposed to be my job. But with school work and all that I aint really have time to plan it. But the next party will be a smash, you can bet on it."

"That's cool, but I have to get invited first."

"Oh, you can bet that you'll be on the V.I.P list."

"Okay, let me know when it happens. I have to go find my roommate."

"All right" he smiled as he ran down the stairs.

"If he was taller hmm"

Gena couldn't wait to get back to the dorm.

She took off her high heels and tossed them on the floor beside her bed before crawling into it.

"That was one of the lamest parties ever. The music was whack, the people were lame and the punch wasn't even spiked. My high school parties were more live than this one."

Gena explained to her roommate.

"I totally disagree, I really had a good time tonight. There were some really nice guys there."

"I saw this cute guy, but he wasn't tall enough for me."

"How tall was he?"

"Maybe 3 inches taller than me and I am 5 ft 6. I want somebody at least 6 feet tall."

"If he treats you right go for it. Height isn't everything right?"

"I guess that's true. He was really sweet too. I think I like him, but we only talked for a few seconds."

"When you see him again, go for it."

"No, I have had enough of that. I wanna try something different this time. I want a guy to talk to me first instead of me having to chase after him."

"That sounds like a really good plan. You should really go with that."

The following day, Gena was walking out of her math class with a classmate,

they had been laughing for the last ten minutes at the professor. While erasing the board,

he sneezed and passed gas all at the same time. The class all laughed so hard that he had to dismiss them right away.

"I'm telling you G that shit was deadly." Tyrone informed her.

"Oh stop lying, we sit in the back, it didn't even reach that far." Gena laughed.

"I think yo nose is stopped up or something because I smelled it loud and clear."

After saying goodbye to her friend, Gena went out to her car.

She was putting her backpack into the backseat when she heard someone come behind her.

She turned around and saw the guy from the party.

"Oh, it's you... hi" she smiled.

"And it's you, how you doing Beautiful one?"

"I am great, just heading to the library to do some studying.

I am amazing myself each day. In high school I never studied, but here I do nothing more than study."

"Oh that's all right, college seems to bring out the best of us. What are you majoring in?"

"Actually sociology I want to learn about people and our cultures and different problems that each cultures face. And it's very interesting so far."

"Watch out now, you gon have your own talk show or something one day."

"I wish, what is your major?"

"I've changed mine a couple of times. First I wanted to do the whole music thing, but I wanna go beyond that and do film production."

"Cool... oh my god, we have been talking all this time and I don't even know your name yet."

"Oh, its Cameron, and yours is?"

"I am Gena"

"Well the pleasure is all mine Ms. Gena. I am ready to know everything about you."

"Why?"

"I think I'll be very impressed when I do."

"Sounds good, but um no thanks. I have to go; my roommate is meeting me there."

"Can I come along, I gotta study too. Maybe I can just study you the whole time."

Gena couldn't help but laugh.

"Stop it, I really have to go."

"Okay, but I won't be so easily persuaded the next time we see each other."

"Deal"

She got into the car and he closed her door for her. She waved as she drove out of the parking lot.

Gena thought about Cameron all that night. He was the first guy that made her feel good about herself. He made her feel like she was really special and worth more than getting into bed with. She wanted him as bad as he wanted her. So she concluded, she would stop playing hard to get and see what he was really all about.

A week went by and Gena didn't run into Cameron not even once.

After a while she gave up on the idea. She was always looking over her shoulder to see if he was around her.

Saturday while walking to her room, someone called her name

She turned around and there he was. A smile appeared on her face. She was so happy to see him.

"What are you doing here?" she said as they hugged.

"Truth be told I was looking for you. I haven't seen you in over a week."

"I know, where have you been?"

"Oh, you missed me huh"

"I didn't say that"

"You didn't have to; body language tells a lot about a person."

"Yeah right"

"Where are you coming from?"

"I went to the mall and bought some shoes. My parents sent me some spending money."

"Oh so you're spoiled like that?"

"I am the only child so what do you expect."

"What are you about to do now?"

"I don't have any plans, do you?"

"I can make up some real fast."

"That doesn't seem to surprise me at all. What is it that you want to do?"

"We can go get something to eat, take a walk, or I can just hold you and tell you how good you look."

Gena smiled, he was not the best at spitting game, but he was so cute.

She had to give him an A for trying.

They ended up going to a quiet little bar. Gena ordered a drink while Cameron admired her.

She decided to speak on it after a while.

"Why are you looking at me like that? "she quizzed her date.

"I can't admire a fine woman when I see one?" he answered her question with another question.

"You can do whatever you want to."

Gena was in heaven at the end of their date. He was so sweet and wanted to know everything about her. This was the first time any man took the time to get to know her. She felt really wanted.

They arrived at the dorm room after 9. Gena had every intention on inviting him in and giving him whatever it was that he wanted. Paula was away for the weekend visiting her parents, so she didn't have to worry about her disturbing them.

Gena opened the door to the room and invited him in. Cameron took off his jacket and tossed it on the bed.

"Where your roommate at?" he asked.

"She is with her folks for the weekend. I have the room alone for 2 days. Do you want a soda or anything?"

"No, I want something else though."

"And what might that be?"

"I'll show you."

He leaned over and kissed her in her mouth. Gena grabbed the back of his head then she kissed him as if she would swallow his tongue.

Once he was satisfied from kissing her, Cameron stopped. Gena looked up at her date.

She never had a guy stop this early in the game. Maybe he needed a condom and wanted ask her if she had one. Or maybe he wanted to do some more foreplay first.

"Ima go ahead and go to the crib. Can I give you a phone call later on?" he asked her.

"Why are you leaving so early? I told you we have the place to ourselves."

"I don't really think this is a good idea."

"Oh, you don't want me. I don't blame you. I aint stupid, I know you probably heard what them niggas said about me."

"That's one thing I don't do, and that's believe in rumors. I rather find out the truth on my own."

"Well why are you leaving like you are turned off all of a sudden?"

"Because I wanna get to know you, we aint gotta have sex already. It should be special.

Just like you are." He kissed her on the forehead then headed to the door.

Gena and Cameron became one of the most talked about couples around campus.

He treated her like a princess and every guy knew she was his girl. Gena was so happy with Cameron.

However, her grades started to decrease because she spent all of her free time with him.

They got their progress reports in November. They decided to open them together at his place after school. Cameron had all A's and one B minus.

"What you get," he asked her?

"Who cares? Just take off those pants and that shirt" she demanded him.

Gena was addicted to this man. He had a loving so intense that she would climax at least twice every time they made love.

"Not right now. Let me see yo grades."

She sighed and tossed the piece of paper onto his lap. Cameron was pissed when he saw her

Progress report.

"What the hell are you doing in school?" he questioned her.

"Huh?" she said pretending to not know what he was asking her.

"You got like 5 D's in all your classes and one C minus. Do you need a tutor?"

"A tutor? I'm not some dumb ass chick. I just haven't had time to do my assignments."

"And why not?"

"Because I am too busy spending my time with you."

"I love you and I wish I could spend every minute of the day with you. But I can't and school is very important to me. And you should feel the same way. Baby you gotta do better. You won't get a good job with grades like that."

"Well I don't care about no job."

"Yeah, I forgot that you're rich and your parents will take care of you. My folks aint got it like that. So in order for me to survive and live comfortable, I gotta do good in school."

"I never said my parents are gonna take care of me for the rest of my life."

"But they won't let their little girl suffer."

"Are you gonna help me with my homework?"

"Sure"

She smiled and leaned over to kiss him.

Gena kissed Cameron once more before getting into the car. It was Thanksgiving break and she was going to spend the week back home with her parents. Cameron would stay there and do some extra credit for one of his classes. Gena begged him over and over to come home with her.

However, he knew there would be no way that he would be able to keep his hands off of her even around her parents.

"I will call you as soon as I get to the house. Gosh Cam, I really wish you would come with me" Gena said with a frown on her face.

"I told you that I'll be fine here. Go spend some time with your people.

I'll be right here when you get back."

"I love you so much."

"I love you more than you could ever love me."

She wrapped her arms around his neck. They stared into each other's eyes then he gave her a passionate kiss.

She drove home for the first time. Gena played some of her new cassette tapes that Cameron made for her a few days ago. The drive turned out really fun. She made it to the house in less than three hours. Tangie and Charles were waiting on the front porch when she pulled into the drive way. She had called them just five minutes ago at a pay phone. She knew her parents were hardly home, and wanted to make sure someone would be there when arrived.

Gena hugged her mother then her father.

"You look like you have put on a few extra pounds sweetie." her mother informed her as she looked her up and down.

"No, I am still the same size I was when I left Mommy." Gena replied trying to not sound so sarcastic.

She loved her parents very much, but sometimes they wanted too much from her.

"Where are your bags dear?" her father asked to change the subject.

"They are in the backseat." Gena informed her dad.

Tangie rubbed the small of her daughter's back as they headed into the house.

Being home was so different for Gena. Her room looked like it belonged in a showroom somewhere. She had almost forgot how rich she was. The house was quiet today. And there was nothing for her to do. Whitley was on a family cruise for the holidays, Shantale was spending some time with her sister. Gena was pretty much alone for the week. She missed her girls so much. So much had happened to her since she went off to school. She wanted to let them know about Phillip and how he played her. She wanted to tell them about Cameron and how he was her true love. There was no one to talk to.

Gena and her parents tried to make sure her stay was a good one. They took her shopping, to a

Concert, and to a play. Sunday they got dressed up and went to an expensive restaurant for dinner.

Gena felt a certain way about being there. This was her life, but she wanted a change.

"Tell us about school GeGe. How are your grades, your roommate, have you met some decent friends?" Charles asked his daughter.

"My grades are fine, and my roommate is cool. She is in Mexico for the holidays." Gena replied.

"How are your classes thus far?"

"They are interesting"

The food came out later. Gena felt so much better when her plate came. For some reason she felt like she hadn't eaten in days.

Charles watched as his daughter ate her meal like she was starving. Just as she finished her food,

a nauseous feeling overpowered her, and she ended up throwing up all over the table.

Charles hopped up and placed his napkin over it.

"Let's go to the bathroom baby." Tangie said grabbing Gena's arm.

She was so surprised. Where was all this from? She felt fine so there was no reason why she should have threw up.

Tangie washed off Gena's face and dress as if she couldn't do it herself.

"Are you feeling fine? I hope they haven't given you food poison. I am so sorry, are you running a fever?" Tangie asked as she felt her daughter's forehead.

"Mom, I feel fine. There is nothing wrong with me. I guess I just ate a little too much that's all." Gena informed her mother.

"Don't say that, we are taking you to the hospital."

"There is nothing wrong with me. We can just go home, and I will get some rest." Gena tried to convince her mother.

Little did she know that Tangie had her mind made up and the hospital is where they were going.

The doctor smiled once he came into the room with the results.

"Well it wasn't anything she ate, but more like what she did." He spoke up.

"Excuse me Doc, but I don't understand" Charles said.

"Your daughter is 7 weeks pregnant." Doctor Nelson explained.

"Pregnant, are you sure? There has to be some kind of mistake our daughter is in college and we made it very clear to her that she is not to be sexually active." Tangie added.

"Well you will have to discuss that with your daughter, but she is pregnant."

Charles and Tangie were stunned to hear the results. It did make sense thought. Gena had put on a few pounds, she slept all day and she was eating every few hours.

They decided not to speak on the subject until they were home.

Charles called Gena into the living room later on that night.

"Sit down, your mother and I have a few things on our minds that we want to say to you. And we have really thought long and hard about this… so take it the way you want to." Charles added.

"First off I want to know who is the father of your unborn child?" Tangie asked.

"His name is Cameron and we have been dating for a few months now." Gena said proudly.

She knew this would surprise her parents to know she actually had a boyfriend, and hadn't got knocked up by just a random guy.

"Cameron, where is he from, and is he in school?" Tangie quizzed her next.

"Yes, he is in school. He is a really good guy and he really loves me." Gena said next.

"A man will tell you anything just to get what he wants from you. That boy doesn't love you. And what are you doing having sex? We clearly told you to go to school and get your education. We are not spending all this money a semester on your school just for you to sex every Tom, Dick, and Larry that comes around. I have never been so mad in my life! Since this semester is already paid for, I am ok with you going back to school. But your father and I are done. We wash our hands with you. You are on your own, and I hope you and your unborn child the best." Tangie explained.

"You hope us the best? What are you saying?" Gena asked her mother.

"We can no longer deal with you Gena. You are a grown woman. You were big and grown enough to lay down and make that child. So be big and grown enough to raise it." Charles spoke up.

"But I'm only 18 and I can barely take care of myself." Gena started to cry.

"Oh now you're a child huh? Well you should have thought about that before you opened your legs for this so called boyfriend of yours. I love you and we will always love you, but today it ends. We are no longer your source" Tangle said to her one and only child.

"You aint said nothing but a word. Me and my baby will be just fine without either of you." Gena said with tears in her eyes. Usually she would never show her hurt in front of anyone. However these people were her parents and her only support system. She didn't really want an abortion, so she had to face the world and make it on her own.

She went upstairs to pack her things. Since they were done, so was she. Gena promised herself to never ever come back here. As far as she was concerned her parents were now dead to her.

Gena felt tears run down her face. Knowing that she wouldn't have her family's support once her child came really hurt. At least she did have Cameron.

Once all of her things were packed up, she called him. The phone kept ringing as if no one was home. Gena hung up the phone and decided to send Cameron a page. He would usually call her within the next hour. She would wait for him to return her call then leave afterwards. 2 hours passed and there hadn't been any word from Cameron. Instead of waiting any longer, Gena continued to pack and headed back to school, never to return there again.

Gena drove straight to Cameron's house. She knocked on the door as hard as she could. Mad would be an understatement to describe her feelings at that moment. This was the one time that she needed him the most. She was carrying their child, her parents now disowned her, he was ignoring her calls and her pages.

Finally one of Cameron's roommates opened the door. He had this cold look on his face when he realized It was her the whole time.

"Where is he? I have been calling his ass all week, where he at" Gena started to go off?

"He aint here Gena" the guy simply replied.

"Where is he then?"

"He aint here, just go home and get some rest."

All of a sudden this power overcame her. She pushed Micah out of the way and rushed into the house.

"Cameron bring your lying ass down here now! I know you are in here somewhere." she shouted.

Micah grabbed her and headed out of the living room.

Gena started kicking and trying to pull him off of her. She had no intentions on leaving that house without at least talking to him first.

"If you don't want what Cam is about to get then you better put me down right now." she explained to him.

Micah finally let her go. He looked like he had something on his mind.

"Gena you better sit down." he said with this awful look on his face.

"Just go ahead and tell me. He is with some other broad right?" Gena shocked him and said.

She was trying her best to keep the tears from coming.

"No, Cameron isn't here Gena. He would never hurt you like that. And that dude loved you. He talked about you all the times." Micah said with tears forming in the corner of his eyes.

"What are you talking about, what do you mean by he loved as in past tense?" Gena said, searching his eyes.

"He was killed at a party last night." He informed her finally.

There was no way she would ever believe him. Gena knew her man he was there somewhere, and she wasn't leaving until he came down.

"I don't know what stupid ass games you and Cam are playing, but it's not funny! He better come down here now! I just had the worst vacation in my freaking life. I am pregnant with his baby, my parents have decided to disown me, and now he is trying to ignore me."

"I wish I was lying to you. He didn't even make it to the hospital." Micah said as tears slid down his face. At that moment she knew he was telling the truth.

"You... so you're telling me my boyfriend is gone? I mean... gone, like I wont ever get to see him again?"

"Yeah, I told him not to go! But he said he was bored here, and he couldn't stop thinking about you. So he went to get out the house."

"No!!!" she started crying.

Micah grabbed her and held her close. He knew her pain, he had lost his best friend as well.

Gena was lost for words after hearing the news. She told Micah she was sorry before leaving.

Once Gena got to her room, she dropped her things onto the floor and walked over to her bed. She kept seeing Cameron's face in her head. She flopped down onto her bed and burst into tears. Just the idea of never ever seeing his handsome face again was unbearable.

Why did she have to lose everything all in one day? Life didn't seem worth living after that.

On the day of the funeral Gena went to a movie and dinner. She knew she couldn't face him. It was after 10 when she got back to the room that night.

Paula was there, she had attended the funeral.

"Hey," she said as Gena walked into their bedroom.

"Hey," Gena said in a low voice.

"Everybody asked about you. I told them that you needed your rest. And some wanted to let you know that they are praying for you."

"How was the service?"

"It was really beautiful. Cameron looked like he was just sleeping."

Gena flopped down on the bed and burst into tears.

"I'm sorry, but I am not good with losing loved ones. I lost everything and when I thought things couldn't get any worst, my man dies."

"I am so sad for you. You didn't deserve to lose anything." Paula said as she hugged her friend.

"I may as well leave now. I won't be able to afford school on my own plus take care of my unborn child"

Gena confessed.

"Whatever you need don't be afraid to ask me."

Gena packed up all her things there. Then she said her goodbyes to some neighbors. After that she headed for a hotel. She had no idea how her life was about to change forever.

CHAPTER 14

Reunited

Dandra went home for her brother's big game. His team was in the finals and he had won the trophy for the Most Valuable Player. Dandra couldn't be prouder. He was her little brother, but she raised him more like he was her son. Their mother was always working so Dandra was the only mom they really had. After the game, she took him to a local bar to celebrate.

At only 20 years old, he had several NBA teams watching him and he was even up for draft.

"I couldn't be more proud of you. You are the man around town. Just keep your head focused and you will go so far. Have you thought about what NBA team you want to go with?" Dandra asked her little brother.

"No, whatever team has the best money offer is the one I'm going to pick." he replied.

A girl walked by, she was young, and very attractive. She smiled and waved at Darius.

"Please make sure you are extra careful when it comes to women. Most of them are just after a dollar and not you. And they will sue you for almost anything these days." Dandra explained.

"I got this, how long are you gonna be in town?"

"I am leaving out tomorrow night. I have a few things I have to do back at home."

"Why did you move so far away from us?"

"Because my life wasn't that great growing up here. It seemed like every bad thing that could happen it did to me. So once I graduated from high school I left."

"It aint that bad around here, but I aint trying to stay around here either."

"Is somebody sitting in this chair?" a man asked Dandra?

She turned to see a very attractive face. The only problem was he was no random guy.

Kyle sat on the bench with his two children. He checked his phone once more to make sure the time on it was correct. Yes it was really 4:13pm. Where was she, they agreed to meet at the park at exactly 4pm. Just when he was about to leave, a luxury car pulled up into the parking lot. The driver's door opened and this stunning woman stepped out.

Sure enough it was Whitley. She looked as if she had just stepped off of someone's run way.

Kyle stood up to greet her with a hug. She was dressed in a white and red pant suit.

Her hair hung gracefully down her back and her face had just the perfect amount of makeup on it.

Kylie looked up, when she realized this was her mother she got up and ran full speed towards her. A smile appeared on Whitley's face. She wrapped her arms around her daughter as if she didn't plan on ever letting her go.

Whitley wiped her eyes then she held Kylie's hand as they walked over to her husband and son.

"Mommy, I missed you so much. We thought you were dead." Kylie said to her.

"No, baby... Mommy just had to go away for a while to get better." Whitley informed her daughter.

"I thought you was gonna stand us up. How are you?" Kyle said to his wife.

"No, my hair appointment lasted a little longer than expected. How are you," she replied?

"I'm living, you look very beautiful." he complimented her.

"Thank you, hi K.J are you going to say hi to your mommy?" Whitley quizzed her son.

He stood up and gave her a hug. He was shy and for the last 2 years Daddy was the only mother he knew.

"I thought since its getting late we could go to the house and talk over dinner." Kyle suggested.

"Sure, I can do that." she smiled.

Whitley was very surprised to know that they were back in the same house. She thought they would have moved somewhere across town.

"When did you move back here?" she asked him.

"A month after you left. The kids missed the house so I thought it would be best to move back." Kyle explained.

"I am glad you did. It looks really good in here."

"I did a few changes, but its home. I'm making chicken is that ok with you?"

"Yes, anything is better than hotel food."

While Kyle was in the kitchen cooking, Whitley decided to have a talk with Kylie. They were in her bedroom. Instead of the old Hello Kitty decorations on her walls, Kylie decorated her walls with pictures of her favorite singers and rappers. This one little boy stood out, he was very cute with long cornrows and these hazel eyes. The name under his posters read Lil Bow Wow.

Whitley smiled because she knew her daughter was growing up.

"I wanted to first tell you how sorry I am for leaving. Sometimes as a grown-up we do things we shouldn't do, and then we have to live with the outcome. It's like if you did something bad and Daddy spanked you or punished you. Well it's different when you become an grownup. When you do bad things to others, bad things will have to you, it's called karma. And she is quite the… never mind. I am just blessed that I am back, and I get to see your pretty little face again." Whitley said playfully pinching her daughter's cheek.

Kylie laughed then she decided to ask her mother another serious question.

"What did you do?"

"I hurt Daddy's feelings. But enough about all of that. I just want to enjoy being home."

"I thought you were dead. Daddy said he you were sick, then he just started saying that he didn't know where you were."

"Well I am not sick anymore, and I promise you that I will never ever leave you the way I did before."

Dinner was great, but awkward for them both. They were a married couple that felt like they were strangers. Kyle put the dishes into the dishwasher once dinner was over. Then the kids insisted that they watched Shrek as a family.

The kids were laughing every few minutes, Whitley even found herself laughing a few times. Eddie was hilarious, and donkey was by far everyone's favorite character.

Kyle brought them a bowl of popcorn and some sodas. After a while it started to feel like home again.

The cheating, him leaving, and the kidnapping all disappeared for a while. The only thing that Whitley could think of was her handsome husband and their beautiful children.

The movie soon ended, and it was bedtime for the kids. Kylie wanted her mother to tuck her in so she did. Kylie looked up at her as Whitley pulled the covers up to her neck.

"Shrek is so funny huh mommy" Kylie chuckled.

"Yes, he is" Whitley smiled.

"I miss watching family movies with you and Daddy. We always laughed because Daddy has the silliest laugh."

"I heard him tonight, he sounds like a wounded bear." Whitley laughed just thinking about it.

"He does (chuckles)… Are you staying here with us tonight?" Kylie wanted to know.

"Right now your father and I are not on good terms. I am staying at a hotel. But if possible I will come and see you guys every single day. Would that be ok for now, just until your father and I sort some of our issues out?"

"Okay, I'm really happy you are here."

She gave her daughter a kiss.

"I love you and your brother more than I love myself. I am here to stay even though your father and I might live in separate homes right now."

"I love you too Mommy."

Kyle smiled when Whitley came back into the living room.

"Hey, do you have a few minutes to talk to me?"

"Yeah, what is it?"

"I wanna thank you first off for coming by tonight. The kids needed to see you. After a while we started to believe that you were gone for good. I am happy that you are back. And I know things ended badly between us, but I think we still have to be cordial for the kid's sake. This may sound all of a sudden, but I have the divorce papers ready." Kyle said.

Whitley felt like a knife had just stabbed her right in the chest. She hadn't been home for 24 hours yet, and he was already filing the divorce.

To make him happy she went ahead and signed them. He smiled as he folded the papers up. There must have been a special lady in his life.

After all of that Whitley got ready to head home. She had experienced more excitement than intended. Kyle felt somewhat relieved once Whitley signed the papers. He once loved her with his whole heart and soul, but she hadn't did the same for him. He often wondered when did she stop loving him.

Was the other man really worth her losing everything over? There was no way he could forgive her and after a 2 year separation he knew it was best to divorce and never look back.

Gena drove her car to her parent's ranch. She was lucky to find her car at a pound not far from the hotel she left it at. Her parents gave her the money to get it out.

She exhaled and prayed that everything would go all right at this meeting. Gena hadn't seen her babies in over a year.

Camrey froze when her mother walked into the house.

"It's me, oh my goodness, look at you." Gena said smiling at her oldest and only daughter.

She opened her arms as wide as she could and hugged Camrey as if she didn't plan on ever letting go.

The two of them cried as they were reunited. The boys ran in and joined in. Gena laughed and wiped her eyes.

"I missed all of you so much. My baby is so big, wow." Gena smiled.

"Where have you been? We thought you was dead." Camrey spoke.

"I was away trying to get myself together. I wasn't the best mommy to y'all, and I promise to do better."

Gena explained.

After taking the kids to the park and to lunch, Gena came back to meet with her parents.

"Your father and I have been talking, and we feel like you should stay here with your children and get to know them until you're on your feet again." Tangie explained.

"I won't be here too long. And I am looking for a job." Gena replied.

Camrey and Gena shared a bedroom. After her bath, Cam hopped into bed with her mother.

She hadn't been this happy in so long.

Gena wrapped her arms around her baby girl.

"I thought about you every day. When people told us that you were dead I didn't believe them. I knew you would come back. But why did you leave us?" Camrey asked.

"I was having some real issues that I had to deal with. I am home for good so you aint gotta worry anymore."

"Are we gonna live with grandpa and grandma forever?"

"No, just until I can get a decent job and a new place to stay and in a nice area. No more places in the hood."

"I really like them; they give us whatever we ask them for."

"And you deserve that."

"I thought you said they were dead."

"To us they were, and I don't want you to start hating them because of me."

"You can tell me."

"When I went to college they made a deal with me. If I kept good grades, didn't mess around, and stayed focus on my school work they would take care of me for the whole 4 years. But I met your daddy and fell in love. On Thanksgiving break I came home sick and they found out I was pregnant. So they told me that since I disobeyed them I had to move out and I had to take care of myself. I also had to go back to school to tell your father the news. But when I got back there his friend told me he was killed at a party just the night before. Not only did I lose my family that week, but my soulmate. I love my parents but I can't help but blame them for everything. They shut me out when I needed them the most." Gena came clean. She had to end the conversation because she knew if she didn't she would start crying.

"I didn't know, I am sorry Mom. What was my daddy like?

"He was very handsome, funny, sweet, and he was so smart. He knew how to treat me. When we were together nobody else mattered. You have his gorgeous eyes and smile."

"Would you have married him if he was still alive?"

"Of course, we would be living in a 3-story home and you would probably have more siblings running around." Gena chuckled.

Shantale wore one of Angelica's colorful sundresses and some pretty sandals to church that

Sunday. Toris' car was parked in the pastor's parking space as it did every Sunday. She took a deep breath as she headed inside. She knocked on the door that stood in front of his office. He opened the door seconds later. Seeing her face to face almost felt unreal. She still took his breath away with her beauty. Out of the thousands of women he ran into all the times, none of them made him feel this way.

"Hi, can I come in?" she asked shyly.

"Sure," he replied

Shantale took a seat in a chair that sat in front of his desk.

He fixed his tie as he sat back down.

"What can I do for you?" he asked her.

"The last time we saw each other things didn't end so well. So if you don't mind, I would love to start over with you." Shantale explained.

"Sure, we can do that."

"My name is Shantale Atkins. I was the first of the two kids my parents created together. It was my father, my mom, and my baby sister Angelica. We had everything, even though my father was away most of the times traveling with his jazz band. Life was perfect, until I was ten years old. My father was killed while on tour that summer. That was the worst day of my life. Not only did I lose my father… but a part of my mother died with him that day. Things were different at home; my mom was often gone and me and my sister had to figure out things for ourselves. My father did leave us over five million dollars in insurance money. My mother made sure we dressed to impress; I drove a 30k dollar car in high school. In 1987 I graduated from Downer High. The day of my high graduation the bank called and said if we didn't pay almost ten thousand dollars they would foreclose on our home. My mom had been on drugs ever since my father died. I remember TVs used to come up missing, her expensive paintings,

our designer clothes and bags. Then I figured it out one day when I found a pipe under her sink….

With that being said, there was no money left for me to go to college. And where we were from If you didn't go to college there was only two ways to make money; prostituting, or the local clothing factory. So I met a friend who introduced me to stripping. I did it because it was fast money and it was the only job I knew that could support me and my sister. Then one day I met the man of my dreams. He came in and literally swept me off of my feet. I couldn't dare tell him that I was a stripper paying for my college tuition. That is why I lied to you, I wanted to keep you interested in me.

I never meant to hide it from you. I just wanted to do whatever it took to keep you in my life." Shantale confessed.

Toris paused for a second then he decided to speak.

"Pleasure to meet you… I must admit that I was torn apart when I found out the truth. And what hurt the most was I asked you were you hiding anything from me, and you said no. Did you honestly think I would love you less if I knew you stripped to get through school?"

"Honestly, I did, you were perfect. And I came into your life with all of my flaws. I thought I had to pretend to be something I wasn't to make you stay."

"Being a man of God, I have learned some wisdom. If God intended on us being together, nothing could have stopped us from being with each other."

"I didn't know that at that time."

"Are you hungry?"

"A little, why did you ask?"

"Let's finish over dinner please."

"I came in Angelica's car."

"Ok, follow me to the restaurant then."

He stood up and she followed him out of the office.

The two ended up at their old favorite soul food restaurant, "Mary Lou's".

Toris couldn't stop staring at Shantale as she looked over the menu. She was so beautiful, and he was so attracted to her. If only she knew how bad he missed her. Every Sunday he would look out into the audience just to see if she was there. All she had to do was say she wanted to come home and he would let her with open arms. He had forgiven her a long time ago for hiding her past from him.

The food was delicious, and they were both satisfied with the meal.

"Would you like some dessert?" Toris asked her.

"No thanks, I've had enough" she smiled.

"Ok, what's next?"

"I have to get Angelica's car back to her, but I need to stop by the house and pick up a few things first."

"All right, we can head there now."

Toris left some bills on the table before escorting Shantale out of the restaurant.

She followed her husband inside their once happy home. It was still the same way it was when she left. It smelled like fresh pine sol. Toris followed her up to their master's bedroom. She looked around to see if anything was out of place. Toris would never cheat on her, but her mind still made her look around to see if anything was out of place.

"I just need some outfits and some shoes for work." Shantale spoke.

"Go ahead they're your things" Toris assured her.

He watched her grab things, bend over, reach up in their walk-in closet. It had been such a long time since he felt her. He needed her; he could almost taste her good loving.

He walked into the closet over to where she stood.

"Let Daddy help you" he spoke.

Then he placed her hands into his and softly kissed them.

"I missed you and I never stopped loving you. You're Mrs. Atkins forever." he promised her.

Shantale looked up at him. He was making her so weak that she could barely stand.

The next thing she knew was Toris has his tongue down her throat. They kissed and kissed.

Then he pushed all of her jewelry off of the shelf and then sat her on top,

Shantale started ripping his clothes off of him and he did the same for her.

"I need your love; I crave for it." she moaned.

In the next few minutes he was giving her the business like she had never had it.

CHAPTER 15

The second chance

Dandra stood up and told Darius to do the same. He gave her a funny look.

"Let's go this place just became a little too crowded." she said loud enough so that Spencer could hear her.

"What did I do to you that made you hate me for over ten years?"

"Nothing, all you have done was cheat on me with two scanks on our graduation day." She snapped.

"If you would just let me explain what happened. I have been trying to find a way to tell you this for a long time." Spencer admitted.

"Darius take my car home, I'll have Spencer drop me off at the house later on."

She had to admit how handsome Spencer had turned out. Where they came from if a guy started off cute he would end up ugly. Doing drugs, alcohol, and being with all types of women were a few bad things their men had to encounter.

Dandra followed him out to his Cadillac Deville. He started the engine and they were on their way. He took her to his house. It was once his grandmother's but once she passed it became his. Dandra couldn't help but think back to all the memories she had once shared with Spencer in the very same home.

"Can I get you something to drink or eat?" he asked while taking off his jacket.

"No, I am just fine."

"How long are you in town?" He joined her on the sofa.

"Just for a few days. Darius did great in the finals, so I came to support him."

"That's cool, he was big man on campus."

"I am really proud of him."

"Yeah, you were like his mom growing up."

"He is my baby"

"How often do you come into town?"

"Years at a time, there is nothing here for me."

"Now tell me again why you hate me."

"On graduation day I realize we were both busy, but my mom got arrested and it just put a damper on everything. But I was coming over to ask you to take me downtown to get her, and before I could get close enough I saw you on your porch kissing Angela.

Then I went to the movies later on with Keri. We went to use the bathroom, and while I am wiping myself… I hear Whitley crying and she confesses to her evil ass friends that she slept with you at the lake. How could you betray me that way? I thought we had really had something special.

But to do something that low to me, I knew we didn't have anything more than a teenage love affair." Dandra explained.

"Ok, why didn't you bother coming over to talk to me about it?"

"What in the hell was there to say? You screwed me over in the worst way. I hated you and

I wanted to kill you."

"I messed up and I can't do enough to make you see that. The day of graduation was one of the worst days of my life. You were going one way and I was going another. I didn't get into

Madison. Then Angela came by saying she was going into the army. And that kiss she gave me was a goodbye forever kiss. Then when

I called you, the phone just kept ringing. I even went by the house and you wasn't trying to see me. That night I went to the lake to clear my head. I saw Whitley she was crying. She said her parents were getting a divorce. So I tried to comfort her and then she asked me to make her feel better. One thing went to the next and we ended up having sex. It didn't mean shit and since I hadn't heard from you, I thought we were over. But I never got over you. I tried dating other women, but they never compared to you. Was I wrong for wanting them to be you? I just want you to give me another chance." Spencer explained.

Dandra was now in tears. She waited so many years to hear those words.

"I guess it hurt me so bad because for most of my life I used to feel like a nobody. People made me feel like I was worthless, and then the boy of my dreams askes me out. I started having this new confidence within and I knew I could trust you. Then when you cheated I felt like everything I ever did or went through with you was all for nothing." Dandra explained.

"And I know that, just give me another chance to prove my love to you."

He leaned closer to her, slowly his lips touched hers. Dandra closed her eyes as they kissed each other. All of a sudden her clothes started disappearing. Spencer laid her on her back and placed her legs into the air. As soon as his tongue touched her pearl of love she started going crazy.

It was like old times and her entire body missed him. There had been a few boyfriends in college and in her early twenties, but they hadn't made her feel the way Spencer did.

Ten lustful minutes passed before she came all over the sofa. Before she could stop screaming he was stroking her with his stick of satisfaction.

Spencer kept kissing her lips and neck. This was the best love he ever had hands down. She didn't have to do much but just moan to drive him insane.

It had been a month since Whitley and Kyle filed for their divorce. Truthfully, she was surprised to know that he still wanted one. She thought they would try to work out their issues for the children's sake. Kyle had been taking care of them for over 2 years so she figured he would now need her help. However he didn't seem to have a change of heart just yet.

Then the dreadful day finally came, the day their divorce was finalized. Kyle kept the house and all of the cars. He did do the right thing and decided that they would split custody of the kids.

He also promised to pay her three thousand dollars a month for spousal support until the kids turned 18.

Whitley walked over to Kyle. They were officially single and no longer husband and wife.

"I guess this is it. Thanks for making this easy for me." She smiled.

"Even though our marriage didn't last, overall we had a good ride. And brought into this world two perfect kids" Kyle informed her.

"That is true, I wish you nothing but the best."

"You too"

He reached over and gave her a hug.

Whitley bought a gorgeous condo downtown and started a new job at a great firm.

Life was finally coming together for the both of them. On Monday, she started her new job.

Her boss walked into her office. He was a tall, dark, and very attractive black man.

He was dressed in a gorgeous designer suit. Nothing on him was out of place.

His name was Carlton Edwards, 35 years old, married, an ex-super model from Europe, and the father to a beautiful 3-year-old son.

She couldn't deny that there was a strong attraction between them, and she kept seeing herself sitting on top of him, while riding him at his desk. He was too fine to even be real.

"Mrs. Mowry, I wanted to once again welcome you to the company. This is your first day with us correct" he asked?

"Yes it is and I wanted to say thank you for the opportunity to work with such an prominent company.

You won't be sorry for hiring me." Whitley smiled.

"Well I know I can speak for the entire company when I say we are glad to have you here.

And you are a very beautiful lady."

"Thank you, Sir"

The day went well, Whitley stayed late to finish a few reports. She kept seeing her coworkers leave the building. Since there was no husband to go home to, she decided to drown herself in her work.

Carlton came into her office a few minutes later.

She looked at her clock to see the time. It was now 7:33 pm.

"You're a little work-a-holic aren't you" He teased her.

"No, I just believe in getting my work done." Whitley replied, not removing her eyes from the computer screen.

He walked over to her and sat on the edge of her desk. At first he just sat there and stared at her. Then he got bold and rubbed his hand across her face. Whitley felt herself become moist between her legs. The old her would have stood up, undid her blouse, and give Mr. Delicious exactly what he was looking for. However, the new Whitley knew that would be a bad idea. This man was married, and she lost everything the last time she messed around.

"If it's all right with you, I would really love to get my work done." Whitley said to him.

Gena was blessed with a job at a local market as a store manager. The pay wasn't perfect, but it was a lot better than the money she was used to making at her other jobs.

Today she was running a cash register to cover for an employee that called out for that day. The day was going well thus far. As she placed a new roll of pennies into her drawer, this man walked over to her line. He had a light brown skin tone, a bald head, pretty light brown eyes and was pretty tall. He looked so much like Cameron that it scared her when she saw his face. For the first time in her life Gena was nervous. He was the most handsome man she had seen since him.

The man placed a few things onto the counter.

"Hello, how are you doing today?" she asked him.

"I was having a jacked up day until I came over here and saw your beautiful self. I didn't know they hired models here." he replied.

Gena laughed and shook her head at him.

"That was a corny pick up line. I am sorry, but that was pitiful." she chuckled.

"Let me take you out sometimes." he said next.

"Why do you want to spend your time with me?"

"I think we would look good together." he said giving her a 20 dollar bill for his purchase.

"You don't know me; I might be a stalker on medication."

"Ok, give me the chance to find out then. What time do you clock out?"

"Be here tonight at 10."

"See you later sexy"

"Bye"

Gena was smiling from ear to ear. She hadn't seen a man so fine in all of her life.

Gena got off work at 9 that night. Even though she didn't know the guy from Adam, a part of her hoped he was already outside waiting on her. She even stood around a little while just to make sure. By 9:30 she left finally.

Tangie was drinking a cup of coffee when Gena entered the house.

Living with her parents was different for Gena. She had been on her own since she was 18 and didn't have to answer to anyone. She could stay out as late as she wanted to, invite any man over that she wanted to, and she didn't have to clean up or do what anybody told her to. However, she didn't try to complain. She knew this was a temporary stay and as soon as her money was right she would be out.

"Hey Gena" her mother said as she sipped the hot coffee.

"Hey Ma, what chu doing still up? You are normally sleep around this time of night." Gena replied.

"I have been up waiting on you. Charles and the kids are all asleep. How did your day go at work?"

"It was work, busy busy busy."

"I am proud of you for getting a job. But I have to be frank with you Gena. We gave you the best of the best when you were growing up. I mean we did things just so that you could have a great life. And I never thought my baby would shop at K-mart, let alone become one of their employees."

"I don't work at K-mart Mama." Gena said to defend herself.

"You may as well this job is just like it."

"Well when you have to drop out of college and become a parent you have to take what you can get."

"Let's be real, we informed you on what we expected from you before you went off to school.

So don't make us out to be the bad guy. Did you think we wouldn't keep our word?"

"I don't know, I mean I thought if I did end up pregnant you would make me take care of the kid, but stay in school at least. Y'all didn't just cut me off financially, but in every way. I know I disappointed you, but I really didn't think you would erase me out of your life for making a mistake.

But Camrey was a gift from God. When I went back to school, I found out her father had been killed at a party just the night before. So that little girl is all I have left from Cameron."

"I know, and it was so hard. We thought about you every single day. Sometimes I almost jumped into the car and went looking for you. We didn't know if you were dead or alive. It was hard on us as well

Gena. Your father and I cried many nights just worried sick about you. We prayed that you were ok.

But we raised you to be very independent, and I was confident that you would survive. Then a year ago we get a call that we have three grandkids who are at school crying and have no idea where their mother is. How could we have been so cold to you? Your father and I have been talking. I know we can't take back the years lost. But we want to do whatever we can to help you and the kids. We want to buy you a house for you and the kids."

"Buy me a house?"

"Yes, a house"

"Ma, I can't let you. I have been doing it on my own and I will forever."

"There isn't anything you can say to change our minds. And an realtor is coming by tomorrow to show you some listings."

Gena was in shock. This was a true blessing and she almost didn't believe it.

"Thank you Ma, you really didn't have to."

"I know but we wanted to."

Gena gave her mother the biggest tightest hug ever.

Shantale washed her bowl after having a serving of Special K cereal. School was still out for the summer so she was on a long vacation. She loved this time of year. This is usually when she and Toris would take their yearly vacation. Being there with Angelica and her family was weird. Even though she was her sister; they had only a few things in common. Angelica had an infant that needed her full attention. Shantale didn't have any kids so she wanted to go shopping, to the movies, and out to lunch. So most of the time she tried to read a good book, mostly the bible.

The doorbell rang so she went to answer the door.

Shantale was surprised to see Toris standing there. It was the first time seeing him after the whole sex thing. He rocked her world that day. It was almost scary how good he made her feel. So for the last month she made it her duty to ignore him.

"Toris, hi... come inside" she finally came to and said.

He smiled as he followed her into the house. They took a seat in the living room to talk.

"I'm surprised that you're here. Every time I call or come by you're either sleep or not here." Toris told her.

"Yeah, been really busy" she lied.

"I thought we were done with the lies. School is out so you're not working. So what is it?"

"Ok, I'm scared Toris."

"Afraid of what? My love for you? We have already talked about this. We need to move forward and let the past be the past."

"I am trying to, but I can't help but think about what people will see. How will that look Bishop Atkins marries a stripper turned first lady?"

"Why are you worried about that now?"

"Because it's out now. I don't want to mess up your image. And when it gets crazy I don't want you to regret marrying me."

"I love you; I am in love with you. There will be never be a time that I regret anything about you."

"Are you sure?"

"Unlike you, I have never lied to you." he joked.

"Wow, really Toris" she chuckled.

"No, but I miss my wife and I would really love it if you came home with me today."

"Hmmm, can I think about it?"

He leaned over and kissed her in the mouth as if she was an ice cream cone on a hot July day.

"Ok, let me go get my purse."

Toris couldn't help but laugh at her.

Sunday came and after long prayer Shantale got ready for church. Toris escorted her inside as if she was Ms. America. He had accomplished so much in his life but marrying the woman of his dreams was by far the best one yet. He stood behind the podium to speak to the members, but he wasn't bringing the word today.

"Let the church say Amen" he started.

The audience smiled and most said Amen.

"Today someone very special to my heart will be bringing the message to you all today. Please stand on your feet and help me welcome your first lady and the love of my life, Mrs.

Shantale Atkins. "Toris announced to the church.

Everybody in the church stood up and cheered as Shantale walked up to the podium. Toris softly kissed her lips.

"Please sit down and thank you all so much for the prayers and the support. It is a blessing to be in the house of the Lord one more time. It's been a while since I was last here, and I know you all were wondering where I was. All I can say is God isn't done with me yet. (members started clapping and saying Amen) Today I asked my husband if I could speak to you all today. Let's look to God church...

Father God we come to you as your humble servants. I am ready for all you have for me Jesus. I ask that you take control over me and let your holy spirit lead and guide me as I speak to your sheep. Give me all of your words and none of my own. I ask that you belittle Shantale and fill me up with you God. I thank you father, in Jesus name I pray, amen" Shantale prayed.

She looked out into the audience and sighed.

The crowd was huge, and they were all giving her their undivided attention.

Her sermon had everybody hyped. She came from John 8:3-7. The church was so excited, and they loved the message about not judging God's people because we were all sinners.

Toris was very proud of his wife once church ended.

He gave her a round of applause as they sat in his office afterwards.

"That was very impressive, and I didn't expect you to tell them about your pass." Toris said to her.

"I felt they needed to hear it from me first hand verses someone else who is on the outside looking in.

When that guy came by and told you about me being a stripper, I felt like dying. It was so embarrassing and humiliating all together. I wanted to tell you so many times about it. But it was never the right time" Shantale explained.

"God does everything in due season. If people don't accept your past then they have to take that up with God. I already forgave you and that's the only thing that matters right now."

CHAPTER 16

Still in love

Dandra was home on a Saturday afternoon. There was nothing to do so she put on a movie. She hated being so lonely. A month ago she had the most incredible night of her life with Spencer. She couldn't stop herself from missing him. He was still her first and only love.

2 hours passed before a phone call woke up.

Dandra opened her eyes and reached over to pick up the phone. "Hello?"

"Dan, it's me Spencer"

Hearing his voice woke her up right away.

"How did you get my number?" she quizzed him.

The night of their rendezvous Dandra waited until Spencer fell asleep then she left during the middle of the night. It wasn't that she didn't want to stay or even see him again, but she was a big girl now.

There was no time to get her hopes all the way up by this man only for him to hurt her once again.

"Your brother gave me your number; are you ok with that?" Spencer asked her.

"Its fine, what do you need?"

"I want to see you. I haven't seen you since we had sex that night. I can't stop thinking about you. I mean we had a night full of romance and you didn't even stay for the morning after."

"I didn't expect there to be any morning after."

"Can we meet up somewhere?"

"Uh, when are you trying to?"

"Today at the lake, can you come?"

"I will be there in a hour."

Dandra pulled up at the lake an hour and some minutes later. She had no idea to why Spencer wanted to meet her here and what he wanted to say to her.

She took off her sunglasses and headed over to him. All of her mixed feelings went away as soon as she seen his beautiful face. He had on a nice button up shirt, some designer jeans, and a pair of sneakers.

After all these years he still dressed simple but hip.

Spencer reached down and gave his date a kiss and a warm hug. Then he offered her a seat on the

bench. Dandra crossed her legs and looked up at him.

"You look good, thanks for coming." Spencer said first.

"Thank you, you do too." Dandra smiled.

"I asked you to come because I think we have some things to talk about since the night we spent together. After that night I realized a lot of old feelings started to rekindle. I never stopped loving you, but I love you more now than I did before. I wanna spend every waking hour with you. Even when I'm asleep I want you there just so you'll be close to me. You have always been a good woman to me and sometimes I took you for granted. Now I am a grown man and I would love it if you would do me the honor of being my wife." Spencer expressed.

Dandra searched his eyes. Was he really asking her the big question?

"Are you asking me to marry you? The same as being your wife and living and loving only you?"

Dandra asked.

"Yes, I am ready to make that step and you are the only woman I wanna do this with."

Dandra was so stunned with his comment that she had no words.

"I do love you, but I can't stand to get hurt again."

"I was 17 years old I will never break your heart ever again."

"Ok, then my answer is yes."

He smiled as he pulled the box from his pocket. Dandra swallowed hard once she saw how big the diamond was. He had spent some serious dough on this bad boy. That made her realize he did love her and was very serious about this marriage.

Her fingers began shaking as he placed the ring on her finger.

Once it was on, Dandra looked down at her hand. It was a perfect fit. She kissed him with all her might.

Spencer pulled her down onto the ground and continued kissing her all over. He didn't care if anyone was around or watching. He was in love and the world belonged to them.

Whitley got the kids for a week. Since the judge gave them joint custody, Kyle agreed that they would have the kids a week at a time. This was Whitley's first time having them alone since she came home. A part of her was so excited to have her babies there, then there was that part that dreaded them showing up. The way her life was turning out, it was not what she planned. Who knew she would end up having an affair with her boss, lose her husband and lavish life all because she teased a girl in high school?

Deep down she knew this was all of her fault. She couldn't blame Dandra for any of this.

She was the one who had the affair with her boss. The thing was she was hot and bothered one late night at the office. He came in with dinner and drinks. A few bites of sweet and sour chicken and 3 glasses of white wine later, they ended up all over the office. It was so good that they had to do it once more. That one more time became almost a daily thing. If she could go back she would have never went passed the first drink. People always do things hoping and thinking they are careful enough to not get caught. When they least expect it that's when the secret is uncovered.

Whitley went all out for the kids during their stay. Each day they had something to do. They went to the movies, a few museums, shopping, and skating.

Today was the day that they would head back to Kyle's for his week. Whitley was combing Kylie's hair when the million dollar question was finally asked.

"Mommy why don't you live with us anymore?"

"Your father and I are no longer together."

"Did you get a divorce?"

"Yes, we did"

"Do you hate him now?"

"No, I can never hate your father, we will always love each other because of you and Jr."

"I wish you didn't leave us. I don't like living in two houses."

"I am sorry, I never meant to put you or Kyle Jr. through this."

Once Whitley put the last braid into Kylies hair she sprayed oil sheen onto it. Then she sat back and admired her work.

"Go pack your things up and bring your luggage down. Your father will be here in a few." Whitley informed them.

After the kids went up to gather their things, Whitley went to clean the kitchen. The condo hadn't been clean since the kids were there. She didn't mind though; these were her babies and she just wanted them around.

The doorbell rang as she took the dishes out of the dish rack.

She wiped her hands and went to answer the door. Kyle stood there looking as handsome as he has when they first met. Why can't you see the good you have until you lose it?

"Hi, they are upstairs getting the rest of their things packed. You can have a seat until they come down." she told him.

"No, I can stand, I'm not that old just yet." Kyle smoothly replied with his hands planted inside his pockets.

Finally both Kylie and Jr came rushing down the stairs dragging their suitcases behind.

"Daddy!" Kylie cried

He chuckled as his daughter almost made him fall to his knees when she hugged him.

"Are you ready to head home?" he asked her.

"Yes, I had a lot of fun with Mommy though. We went to this science museum, skating, and to the movies." Kylie bragged.

Kyle grabbed their luggage and headed to the front door.

"Say goodbye to your mom before we leave." Kyle told his kids.

They ran over to their mother and hugged her and placed kisses on her face. Whitley did her best to hold back the tears. Seeing her children leave her even for a week was torture.

She watched as they got onto the elevator and even down in the parking lot. Kyle was a great father. He opened the door for Kylie and even closed it when she got inside. Kyle got into the car and in no time it was heading out of the lot. Whitley closed the curtains and sat there all alone. Kyle looked so handsome today like he did when they first fell in love. He even smelled different, and his arms looked like he had been working out lately. Could it be true? Yes, she was still in love with her husband, ex-husband.

Gena sat in the living room when she heard the knock at the door. She couldn't help but think who could be there so late. She smiled when the handsome man on the other side of the door was revealed.

It was her new friend Jace that she met at her job.

They had talked on the phone every night for the last few weeks.

"Glad to see you made it." Gena said as she crossed her legs once she was sitting on the sofa.

She had on a bath robe and half of her thigh was hanging out of it.

For the first time in her life, she was actually nervous around a man. She didn't know what to say so she sat there and waited for him to speak.

"It's very quiet, the kids must be in bed." he said to her.

"Yes, they have been in bed for a few hours now. We don't stay up past midnight up in here unless we pay at least one bill." Gena informed her guy friend.

"I heard that, you old school huh." Jace laughed.

"I have to be tough; I am both Mom and Dad to these kids."

"Hey, you gotta do what you gotta do."

"I couldn't believe it when you told me you don't have any yet."

"No, it's too expensive to have a baby right now. I wanna save up first then have a few little ones. I want my kids to grow up with more than what I had as a kid."

"First man I have ever heard say that. But answer me this though…

Why are you single? You told me over the phone, but I wanna hear your answer in person."

"I like to chase the women I date. I'm old school and these days women are blunt. They just come at niggas all types of ways. Then they give it up on the first night and end up taking care of him. I like to wine and dine my woman, see where her head is, and if It's worth it, then I go for the goods."

Shantale smiled as her husband walked in from work that evening. They had been so happy since she came back home. Every night he took her out on a date no matter how tired he was from work. Shantale was the luckiest woman on earth.

Toris kissed her before joining her on the sofa.

"How was your day?" she asked as she rubbed his chest.

"I am tired, just wanna lay here in your arms all night." Toris replied.

"That sounds so good to me. We don't have to go out tonight. We can order something and just relax in each other's arms."

"Sounds like a plan. Today Marsha brought in a picture of the new baby. When I say she was a little angel, God is so incredible."

"Aww, I love how you adore kids the way you do. When we ever have some I know they will be well taken care of."

"I've been thinking, I think it's about time that we start planning our family."

"You are ready for kids now?"

"Yeah, seeing that baby did something to me. I think I would love having a little one that I helped create running around here."

"I want a few kids myself, but do you think we are really ready for them now?"

"Yeah, I'm going upstairs to take a shower. Be ready because we start trying tonight."

He kissed her on the cheek before disappearing up the stairs.

Shantale was not going to get pregnant anytime soon. The whole past life fiasco hadn't died down yet. She was just enjoying being back home. She was still young, and they had plenty of time for baby planning.

That night Toris and Shantale went at it three times. Each time was full of love and passion.

The next day, Toris came out of the shower and walked into the walk-in closet to find an outfit.

He got a button up Polo shirt and some khaki shorts.

He went back into the bathroom to get some deodorant and saw that he was out. Quickly he remembered that Shantale had some in her medicine cabinet. He walked over to her side of the bathroom and opened it. Inside was a tube of toothpaste, deodorant, eye drops, and some bottles of medicine. Toris had no idea that she was even on medication. He read the bottle; anger quickly filled his body. How could she be hiding yet another secret from him?

He decided against the deodorant and went downstairs.

Knowing what he just found out, Toris had to pray. He knew that if he told Shantale how he felt while he was still mad, he would probably say something he would later regret. So he let God take control of the situation.

Shantale came home from shopping a few hours later.

Toris decided to prepare lunch for them. She came in once their food was on the table.

He made them cold cut subs, potato salad, and lemonade.

Shantale pulled her seat out and sat down across from her husband. He placed a sub onto her plate then he spooned on some salad.

"I am starving, and it smells so good." Shantale spoke up.

"Eat up, how was shopping with Angelica?"

"It was nice, she found Aiden the most beautiful rocking horse. I remember as a kid Angel had one. She rode that thing every day all day. It brought back so many memories seeing him on it today." Shantale replied.

"I hope you are that excited when we have kids of our own. I'm sorry, I never even asked you if you wanted kids. Do you want kids with me?"

"I do one day"

"That means not right now. Why didn't you tell me this before we started trying?"

"I wouldn't tell you no. I want you to be happy."

"I am happy, but why is it that you don't want kids?"

"Well for one we just got back together, and we should save up first."

"Our bank accounts are very sufficient."

"We are not ready to be parents yet. I am used to being able to come and go when I please."

"I see, so that's why you've been hiding another secret from me?" Shantale searched his eyes.

"What?"

"You don't wanna have kids with me? Is that why you went behind my back and got on birth control pills?"

He tossed her the bottle and then got up from the table.

Whitley ran her hands down her dress once more. She was going to get his attention one way or the other. The dress screamed scank but that's exactly what she was going for. It was this sexy black dress that had a V-neck. It showed her c cup perfectly and with her small waist and perfect hips and backside,

Whitley would turn some serious heads today. She did a full twirl in the mirror and then sprayed on some perfume. Her makeup and hair were just as fierce. After one more check she left to pick up the kids from Kyle.

Kyle opened the door when he heard her knock. He went completely numb when he saw her.

She looked like she was about to audition for either a porn or a hip hop video.

"Hello, Kyle are the kids ready? "she asked in a very sexy tone.

"They... they are Ummm... they should be coming down in a second." Kyle could barely get out.

"Should I wait out here on the steps?"

"Don't be silly, come inside" he smiled.

Whitley smiled and walked into the house. He would be sure to watch her from the back and there was no way he could resist her.

As soon as Whitley entered the living room her whole mood changed. There was this pretty dark skinned younger woman sitting on the sofa. And from the looks of it she had been there for a while.

She had this smooth dark complexion like a milk chocolate, long black hair, and a petite frame, even her bra size was impressive. Her face was simple yet elegant and she looked to be in her late twenties.

She had a small nose ring that complimented her very well.

"Whitley this is Tatiana and Tatiana this is Whitley." Kyle introduced the two ladies.

"Oh, hi... Kyle has told me a lot about you. And you all have beautiful kids together." Tatiana spoke up.

"Kyle can I see you for a minute?" Whitley asked right away.

"Sure, give us a minute Tatiana." Kyle told her.

"Oh, no take your time."

Whitley folded her arms as they walked into the foyer.

"Who in the hell is that slut and why is she here around my kids? You can have one night stands, but you don't have to bring them here!" Whitley snapped.

"First off what you and I had is way over. It stopped being your business the day I got that D.V.D. of you playing ride the bull with your boss. And Tatiana aint just some one night stand. We have been seeing each other for a while now. We are going out as soon as you take the kids." Kyle explained.

"You didn't waste any time moving on did you?"

"Are you kidding me?! You cheated on me for only God knows how long and with whoever else. Then you leave for 2 years not telling us where the hell you were. Then you come back like we would go back to the way we were? Sorry it don't work like that around here. You lost that right a long time ago. Now excuse me my date is waiting." Kyle said then he walked away.

Whitley sighed and held back the tears. It hurt her even more to know this whole situation was her fault.

The kids came down with their luggage soon after.

She wiped her eyes so they wouldn't see her tears. After their hugs and kisses, the three of them left.

That night once the kids were asleep, Whitley sat on the sofa and cried. Her life was awful and didn't seem like it would get any better anytime soon.

Kyle had moved on so fast and here she was still madly in love with him. When had he stopped being enough for her? He was such the perfect father and husband. In the bedroom he had always pleased her even if she had to tell him what she wanted. He knew when she needed some alone time. Every

Saturday morning he would get the kids and take them out for breakfast and to a baseball game or something. During that time Whitley would go to the spa or just sleep in. Why did she have to be so greedy and cheat on him? He had never stepped out on her.

"Mommy, wake up" Kylie said as she tapped on her mother's back.

Whitley woke up and turned to her daughter. She had fallen asleep on the sofa.

"Did you sleep down here last night?" Kylie asked.

"I did, how can I help you?" Whitley replied.

"We want breakfast, I would have fixed us cereal, but you don't have any here."

"I forgot to go by the market on the way over to pick you guys up last night. Get your brother and when

I'm dressed we'll go grocery shopping."

"Okay, can I get some of the chocolate cereal?"

"You can get whatever you want."

The kids were ready within the next hour and so was Whitley. She wore some cute jeans, a tank top and some open toe sandals with a 4 inch heel on them. Her hair was up in a ball and she had on a pair of expensive sunglasses.

They left in her brand new BMW.

In the store, Kylie and Kyle Jr were putting all kinds of junk into the grocery cart.

Whitley only let them eat healthy snacks and meals. However, she had so much on her mind since she

saw Kyle's new girlfriend that she didn't care.

"Kylie, how long has Daddy been with his new friend?" Whitley quizzed her daughter.

"A few months" Kylie answered.

"Is she nice to you and your brother?"

"Yes, she always bring us toys when she comes over."

"Does she ever spend the night there?"

"No, she leaves at night."

"She will never be me, so I don't want you or your brother hanging around her, do you hear me?"

"Yes"

Whitley took the kids out to eat at a wing place that evening. The kids were really enjoying the food and the mini arcade that was downstairs. While the kids played, she did a lot of thinking.

Kyle was really over her. That's why he was so eager to get the divorce. Where had he met this

Tatiana, at a strip club? She looked like she was some wanna be model that nobody wanted to work with. Why was she wasting her time wanting someone who no longer loved her? Whitley realized she had to move on as well. And it wouldn't be hard for her. Men were always after her so once the right one came she would jump at the chance.

This guy walked over to Whitley's table. She was looking down at her freshly manicured nails.

"You dropped your phone." he said as he sat her cell onto the table.

Whitley was ready to go off on the man for touching her things. When she saw his face that all went out of the window.

He was very attractive, and she wasn't about to leave without knowing his name and number.

"Thanks" she said putting the phone into her purse.

"No problem... can I get your name?" he asked next.

"Why do you need my name?"

"I see attractive women a lot, but none quite like you."

"I am Whitley and you are?"

The week with the kids was amazing. She made it her business to be ready for Kyle's return to pick up the kids on Sunday.

She smiled when he entered the house.

"Hey, the kids are in the kitchen finishing up their dessert. I made a apple pie." Whitley told him.

"When did you start baking?" Kyle chuckled Throughout their entire marriage he had done all of the cooking.

"I can cook. I just chose not to." Whitley informed him.

He followed her into the kitchen. Kyle was very surprised when he saw this man at her dinner table.

He was eating a slice of pie with his kids.

"I didn't know you had company." Kyle spoke up.

"Oh, this is my friend Luke. Luke, this is my ex-husband and my children's father." Whitley introduced the two to each other.

Kyle smiled and shook Luke's hand. He didn't seem jealous one bit.

"Ok, guys go get your things together" Whitley told the kids.

"How long have you been going out?" Kyle asked Luke.

"Not that long, we are still getting to know each other." Luke answered.

"Cool, you look good together." Kyle smiled.

"Thanks man, she is a good woman."

Kyle had nothing to say about that one. He used to think the same thing about his wife. Then once the truth came out, he saw her as another backstabbing you know what.

Once the kids and Kyle were gone, Whitley felt bad and wanted to be alone.

She couldn't believe that Kyle hadn't made a big deal out of her date. He was actually happy that she had moved on. Did he hate her that much?

"That was quite a pie. So what do you wanna do now?" Luke asked as he entered the living room.

"Well I have work in the morning. I will give you a call later" Whitley said.

"Oh, I understand, I enjoyed our time together."

"Have a goodnight"

"You too"

Whitley had no intention of calling Luke that night or ever again. He was only bait for Kyle and since that didn't work she was done.

She locked the door after he left, then went upstairs to prepare for bed.

CHAPTER 17

Karma is a Motha

Gena went to Jace's house to spend some time with him on her day off. His place was not decorated too much but it was very clean. He seemed like he was the perfect guy, and Gena kept feeling like he was too good to be true. He called her every day, and when he said he would call her back, he really did. He was always complimenting her and whenever she needed him to come by he would always show up.

"Make yourself at home." Jace smiled at his date.

"Thank you, it's very clean in here" Gena said crossing her legs.

"My mom is my maid... I'm just joking (chuckles) I just got off of work, I'm gonna take a shower and then we'll chill" he informed her.

"Take your time, I'll be here when you get finished." Gena said giving him a sexy grin.

He kissed her softly on the lips and off he went. Gena grabbed the remote for the television and flipped through the channels.

106&Park was on BET. She left the tv on that channel.

"Why is Free still rocking that old air fro? She is too pretty for that." Gena said to the tv screen.

Ten minutes passed and the phone started ringing. Gena had no intention on answering it. Finally the answering machine picked up the call.

"Hey Sexy eyes I am coming into town for a few days and I really want to see you. We have a lot to catch up on. Love you Jace, see you soon."

Gena almost lost her mind. Who was this calling her man sexy eyes?

"Wow, so he has women in and out like that? I can't do it; he can have her and whoever else he got leaving messages on his answering machine."

Gena put her purse on her shoulder and headed for the front door.

Jace came out just as she was turning the door knob.

"Where are you going?" he questioned her.

"I am going home because you are a two timing dog. I heard some broad on your answering machine.

She will be in town soon Pretty eyes." Gena mocked the caller.

"Pretty eyes? Before you go off the handle, that was my cousin Simone. We grew up like sister and brother. She comes into town on business every once in a while. And she always spends time here with me. We are nothing more but kids of two sisters." Jace informed her.

Gena felt like a fool. They weren't even official, and she was already jealous of other women in his life.

"Since you are so hot right now, let's hop into the pool outback." Jace smiled.

"I can sure use a swim."

The two walked out to the back yard. He had this nice pool that was put into the ground a few months ago.

Gena stripped down to her matching panty and bra. Jace was very pleased with what he saw.

She was finer than any woman he had ever seen in person. His flesh was weak, and if he allowed it, they would end up going at it in the pool.

Jace motioned for her to swim to him. Then he put her in his arms. In no time they were sucking each other's face like they never wanted to let go.

After a hour of swimming the two got out to talk. Gena wiped off her body with a dry off towel.

Jace brought her a glass of iced tea.

"Thank you, that swim was magical. I know that sounds crazy, but my body feels amazing now."

Jace sat next to her on the sofa once they had their clothes back on. He put his arms around her waist.

"Did anybody ever tell you that you are sexy as you can be?" Jace asked her.

"I have heard it but trust me it sounds good to hear it over and over again."

"Oh yeah"

Gena got on his lap and took off her shirt. Slowly she started kissing his lips and grinding on him. Once she felt the hardness in his pants she began undoing her bra. He quickly grabbed her hands and pulled her off of his lap.

"What are you doing? I was about to give it to you?" Gena said almost screaming.

"This is not the time for that Gena." Jace said fixing his pants.

"Are you not attracted to me?"

"What the hell? I wouldn't be hard as a rock right now if that was the case. I love everything about you.

But I'm celibate right now."

"Huh?"

"You heard me right"

"Ok, I need some answers… why are you celibate?"

Toris decided to not even speak to Shantale. He knew that if he did he would say something that he would have to apologize for later. He was so hurt and felt betrayed. He took her back after finding out she was a stripper. And lately he was catching hell since everyone knew he had married her. He was getting all types of emails from church members. Pastor friends were taking him out to lunch to tell him he was wrong for marrying a harlet. Then on top of that Shantale was holding back as if she didn't want his seed.

She never told him why, but he didn't care it was wrong no matter what the reason was.

Saturday morning Toris walked into the house with some luggage.

His parents came in right behind him.

"Everything looks lovely son." Catherine said looking around the house.

"Thanks Mom, have a seat. I'll go put your bags upstairs." Toris told his parents.

Shantale walked into the living room to grab a magazine. At first she thought her eyes were playing a cruel trick on her when she saw her mother in law sitting on her on her sofa. After a second look, she realized it was true.

"Well hello Shantale." Catherine broke the silence between the them.

"Mr. and Mrs. Atkins what a surprise. I wasn't expecting you all to be here anytime soon." Shantale said trying to not sound so stunned. However Toris hadn't mention anything to her about his folks coming into town.

"Yes, Toris just picked us up from the airport. I asked him why hadn't you rode with him there and he said you were under the weather." Catherine said next.

"I am ok, where is Toris?" Shantale asked.

"He went upstairs to put our bags into the guest room." Franklin finally spoke.

Shantale excused herself from the room in search for Toris.

She found him in the guest room as they had said. He was putting fresh sheets on the bed. Since he and

Shan were on bad terms this had been his new bedroom.

She folded her arms after closing the door behind herself.

"When were you going to tell me that your parents were coming into town?" she asked him.

"Around the same time you were going to tell me you were on the birth control pills."

"Oh very funny, I don't think you want to play with me right now. You had no right to invite anybody here without telling me first. This is my house too and if you don't start treating me with some darn respect I will make life hell for you."

"You have been doing that pretty well as of lately." Toris barked back.

"Oh... well why don't I just leave then?"

"You are a trip girl. You can lie and do all kinds of hurtful things to me, but if I say the wrong thing I'm some mean monster. Yet you are not the innocent one. And if you keep another secret from me I'll do us both a favor and leave."

Toris was so furious that he left out of the room. He didn't want things to get more out of hand, his mother and father were visiting for crying out loud.

Shantale made a wonderful dinner that night for everyone. Toris usually cooked but when his parents came into town she would cook. She didn't need another reason for them to dislike her. Besides she loved to cook, and it gave her time to think.

"This chicken marinara is very tender and it melts in my mouth." Catherine complimented the food.

"Thank you Mrs. Atkins. Rachel Ray gave me a secret ingredient." Shantale replied.

"How is the congregation son?" Franklin spoke to Toris.

"Church is blessed and we are growing each month. I hope y'all are staying for Sunday's service." Toris looked at his parents.

"You know that we don't have a problem with that. If you want us here then you will have us here."

Catherine added.

"I can't wait, it's been a while since y'all came and heard me do my thing." Toris smiled.

"I know, I hate that we live so far away. We would attend every Sunday service if we could." Catherine said next.

"What brought you guys into town anyways?" Shantale asked her in-laws.

"I was coming to look at this boat for sale." Franklin answered.

"We are all adults here and I think we should be honest Frank. Toris is our son and we deserve to know the answer. We are here because we have been getting all kinds of phone calls and mail saying Toris you married a... how can I say this nicely? Is it true that Shantale you were once a stripper" Catherine shock them by coming out to ask.

Toris coughed, he had no idea this was coming.

"Cat, don't do this right now." Franklin warned his wife.

Toris looked at his wife and gave her a that "I'm-so-sorry-I-didn't-know" look.

"Why not? This time is appropriate if any. And I am very curious. Shantale Please answer me. Were you once a stripper?"

"Yes, I was a stripper before I met Toris and he knows it." Shantale boldly answered her mother in law.

"You told us she was a college student and she was this angel. Yeah the devil's angel." Catherine snapped.

"Excuse me, do not disrespect me in my own home. I know you are my elder you're very much older, but you have crossed the line!" Shantale argued.

"Wait a minute this is getting out of control. Mom, that was uncalled for. I accept her past so should you. I married her, not you or the other hypocrites that seems to have something to say about it." Toris informed his mother.

"I agree Son, Cat that was just awful. You could have asked her in a nicer way. I apologize for my wife's nasty attitude. I honestly think if you could've married Toris you would have your damn self. Shantale again I am so sorry Love. Toris already explained to us that you were only paying for you college education. Cat let's go to bed; you have given us all enough drama for the night." Franklin apologized to his daughter in law.

He grabbed his wife's hand and led her out of the dining room.

Shantale gathered the plates and went into the kitchen without saying a word.

Toris came in right behind her.

"I wanna apologize for my mother's behavior. That was just cruel. But I told you I don't care what anyone has to say or think about our marriage. The only people who matter in this are you, me, and God" Toris assured her.

"I know, but it still hurts. Your mother is treating me like a hooker." Shantale explained she tried hard to hold back the tears.

"Come here Love, I love you so much."

He grabbed her and wrapped his strong arms around her.

Shantale was better that night. She took a long bath and then prayed. After that she got on the family's computer to search the web.

There was an email at the bottom of the screen blinking. She clicked on it to see what it was about.

Dear Bishop Atkins,

It has been an honor of mine to watch you grow from a youth minister to now the bishop of your own church. God has really shined a light on your life. I remember when I first visited your church. It was a third Sunday and you had the people shouting and praising God as if he was the one giving the sermon.

I am writing to you because I have such a concern for you. Your personal life is your own business, but it does affect your flock. My family and I have been members of your church for over 5 years. However when your wife told the congregation about her former lifestyle, I have not been comfortable since. How can your sheep follow you when you are still hanging out with the whoremongers? Yes, they need to be saved and we all need Jesus. But it comes off as if you are saying you can turn those type of women into honest house wives. We all know that that is not true. I am trying to get closer to God, but this entire ordeal has been too much to handle. My family and I will no longer be attending your church. Maybe if you divorce her and actually marry a real woman of the Lord you will gain all that God has for you. Until then be prepared to lose your church family all of us.

Best Regards,

an once faithful church member

Shantale was bewildered by the email. How could people be so cruel and especially when she was woman enough to explain the situation to them? She closed out of the email and turn off the compute. This was something that Shantale feared for her husband. Not only was she hurting but he was too for being in love with her. So many more questions ran through her mind. How many emails and letters had he received about the situation?

How many church members actually left their church?

Before she knew it Shantale was in tears. She got into bed and cried like a newborn baby.

Then at dinner Toris' mother made her feel like a cheap hooker. True some strippers did have sex with guys and even gave them oral pleasures for extra money. But for the most part Shantale made her money from dancing naked on stage a few times a week. And she hated each night that she had to perform. After wiping her face she called Angelica.

"How is it going," Angelica asked her sister?

"Not good at all, it was bad enough that Toris was mad at me about the birth control. But today I go downstairs to get a magazine and guess who is sitting on my white plush sofa?" Shantale quizzed her sister?

"Who, one of the church members?"

"Worse, his parents I mean Frank is amazing, but Catherine is the devil. How can Toris be such an angel and be the son of a bitch?"

"You are crazy, but how was that?"

"She said they were in town just to visit. I kept to myself most of the day. Then I cooked my chicken marinara and everything was going good until the witch asked me about being a stripper. I was so stunned I could have spit. Frank got her together then they went to bed".

"Shut your mouth up right now. What was Toris doing while this was going on?"

"He stood up for me. But it wasn't that special since we were already on bad terms. Then as I am on the computer there is an email at the bottom of the screen. I pulled it up to see that it's a church member who is leaving the church because I confessed that I was a stripper."

"You are making this all up right?"

"I do wish I was lying, but it's so true. I feel so awful right now. I cried for over ten minutes just a minute ago. Was I wrong for telling the whole church?"

"Of course not, what's in the dark has to come to the light. Some people just wanted an excuse to dislike you and leave anyways."

"I just feel worthless right now. I don't know what to do Sis."

"Aww, look we will do lunch just to get your mind off of everything. I love you and it's gonna be all right."

Shantale told her sister that she loved her and then they hung up with each other.

As she pulled the covers back, Toris walked into the room.

"Why are you feeling worthless?" he quizzed her.

Shantale stopped dead in her tracks. She was unaware that he had heard her conversation. So that also meant he knew she had found the horrible email as well.

Kyle looked over at the night stand. It was 3 in the morning and he was not used to getting any phone calls this late.

"Hello" he sounded half asleep.

"Kyle, I need your help. I should call the police but I rather you just come over since the kids are here"

Whitley said, sounding like someone was after her with a knife.

"What is it?"

"Please? If I had someone else to call I would."

"I'm on my way"

Whitley hung up the phone and smiled.

30 something minutes passed before there was a knock at the door.

It was Kyle, he knew Whitley was up to something when he saw what she had on.

He shook his head and followed her inside house. There was two glasses of wine sitting on the table along with burning candles.

"Whitley cut the crap, what do you want?" Kyle questioned her right away.

"I heard a noise in the kitchen, and I can't sleep knowing there is something in there." she lied.

Just to prove a point, Kyle went into the kitchen. Whitley ran over to a mirror to make sure her hair and make-up were still in place.

"Like I thought, there was nothing in the kitchen, or hallway. You call me over here at 3 in the morning and when I get here you're dressed like you are about to pose for Playboy or Victoria Secret. Now if you don't mind, I'm leaving and going back to bed." Kyle told her.

"Please, Kyle don't leave me like this. I can't apologize enough. I am sorry for destroying our family. I love you and I miss you like hell." Whitley said, with tears in the corner of her eyes. She had never in her life begged for anything. Every morning that she woke up without Kyle, she felt like dying.

"You don't get it do you? I loved you with an unconditional love. I never even intended on ever cheating on you. And there were plenty of women and times that I could have. But I loved you. And when someone cheats on you everything y'all have built together goes down the drain. You have wasted enough of my time so goodnight." Kyle made it very clear to her.

A few days later, Whitley was still upset with Kyle for turning her down. He hated her so much and there was no way she would ever love another man. He was her soulmate and she let a stupid affair get in the way of that.

She was walking to her car from lunch when she spotted them. It was Kyle and his new girlfriend. They were feeding each other fruit.

Whitley stormed over to them.

"Is this is why you can't be with me Kyle? Because your too busy playing daddy to this ugly little tramp"

Whitley shouted?!

Kyle sighed and shook his head. He was not in the mood for any of her none sense today.

"How did you even know I was here? Are you following us?" Kyle asked her.

"No, I was on lunch and I spotted you over here. You would rather be with her than put your family back together?"

"Excuse me for a minute." Kyle kissed his date, grabbed Whitley by the arm and walked to the side of the restaurant.

"Get your hand off of me! You are so pitiful; you can stop the front I know you are only doing this to make me jealous." Whitley said getting upset.

"Listen to me cause I'm only gonna say this one more time. What we had is long gone, over, done, complete, and finished so stop trying to break Tatiana and I up. Whatever it is that you try it aint gonna work" Kyle snapped.

"What about our kids, don't they deserve to have us together?"

"Let me ask you this... Did you think about me or our kids once when you were screwing that white man?"

Whitley stood there in silence. There was nothing she could say after that.

"That's what I thought. Now leave here before I really cause a scene."

Whitley walked to her car with tears running down her cheeks. She got into the car and cried her eyes out. There was no purpose of living. He was really over her. How could she ever get over the love of her life? She wished a million years that she could take back all the cheating, all of the lies, and everything that ruined her marriage. That saying you don't know how good you've had it until it's gone really made sense to her now.

After Spencer proposed to Dandra, he thought it would be a good idea for them to move in together. It took her two days to move all of her things in and give some to the Goodwill.

He was so excited to have her there and she felt the same way. Dandra made a romantic dinner for their first night together.

Spencer smiled as he looked across the table to see his fiancée.

"It's finally real, do you think you will stop loving me so much with us living together?" Dandra asked him.

"The love I have for you can only get stronger." Spencer assured her by smiling.

"I never expected to reconcile with you, let alone become your fiancée." Dandra said trying hard not to jump for joy.

After they ate, Spencer decided to slow dance with her.

The next morning, Dandra woke up at 6 am to head to work. For the last 6 years she had been a police detective. She made sure the house was spotless before leaving. Then she walked over to the Spencer's side of the bed. To her surprise he was awake. He had this big smile on his face.

"Off to work huh?" he quizzed her.

"Yes, I am... everything is cleaned, and I should be home by 7 this evening."

"Don't let em work you too hard."

"They get me every time" she chuckled.

"I love you, call me on your lunch break."

"I love you too and I will do that."

Dandra softly kissed his lips then she headed out of the house.

Work was hectic, but Dandra lived for solving cases. She entered the house at 7:20 PM.

Tired would be an understatement to describe how her body was feeling. Spencer was on the sofa watching a football game. The TV was up loud, and he had a bowl of potato chips on the coffee table.

And half of the chips were spilled on the floor.

"Hey sexy, how was work?" Spencer asked his fiancée.

"Hello, how was your day at work?" Dandra questioned him back.

From the way things looked he hadn't left the house.

"Uh, it was cool, go shower and come join me." he insisted.

Dandra sighed and then went into the bedroom. The room was in a mess. There was a pile of clothes on the bed, shoes were all over the floor and the bed hadn't been made up either.

Dandra almost screamed when she saw the mess.

After her shower, she took her time and cleaned up the room. There was no way she would go to bed in a dirty room. Once the room was clean, she went into the kitchen. Dirty dishes filled the sink, snack bags were left empty on the counter tops and then an empty bottle of Coke sat there too.

Dandra shook her head and cursed under her breath. She tossed everything into the garbage can and then wiped down the counter top. Her home didn't look this bad after her wildest parties. Dandra almost started regretting leaving her 200,000 dollar home to move into her fiancé's 60,000 dollar one.

Sure the house was in great condition, but it was too small. To top it off she felt like Spencer should have more love for his grandmother's home.

He walked into the kitchen to get something to drink.

"Hey what's for dinner?" he quizzed her.

Was this how her life would be if they got married?

Was this the life she wanted?

CHAPTER 18

Love in all the wrong places

Whitley ran out to the car. It was late Friday and she was keeping the kids while Kyle took a trip on business. When she entered the house, Kyle was sitting on the sofa with his head down.

"Kyle" Whiley called his name. She knew right away that something was wrong with him.

He looked up at her, his eyes were filled with tears.

"You are really making me nervous Kyle, what's the matter?" Whitley asked, sitting down next to him.

"I'm cool" Kyle finally spoke.

"I know you better than that. What is wrong with you?"

"Tatiana broke up with me. Are you happy now?"

"You too were so in love." Whitley said being sarcastic.

"I aint got time for the smart comments."

"I am sorry, what happened?"

"She got back with her ex-boyfriend."

"Is there anything that I can do for you?"

"No, am I that bad?"

"What?"

"I can't seem to please my women. You cheated, then she left me."

"Trust me you're not the one with the problem. When I cheated it wasn't because you didn't satisfy me.

I was just being greedy and thought I could handle being with the both of you. I thought I would never lose your love. Then when I did, I really lost everything."

"Tatiana made me forget about all the pain. I was finally getting over you."

"You'll never know just how sorry I am, but if you need me I am always here for you."

She got up and took the kids out to the car.

Kyle was in pain. True he liked Tatiana, but she was just a cover up of his true feelings. Truthfully, he was still in love with Whitley. However, they had too many issues and he could never trust her again. Whitley did act as if she had learned her lesson, but they were divorced now. The way she hurt him; some people could never forgive. Then again no one had a love as strong as theirs. Plus it was so complicated taking the kids to and from her house every other week. A change would soon come.

After watching Toy Story 2 with the kids, Whitley turned in early that night.

She was sleeping peacefully when she heard someone bang on the front door.

It was only 9:24 pm when she looked over at the alarm clock.

She quickly wrapped herself into a bath robe and then went to answer the door.

It surprised her to see Kyle standing there.

Then he did the unthinkable and grabbed her face, he kissed her like he missed her.

Whitley knew she was dreaming, but since this wasn't real she slid her tongue into his mouth and let it dance around with his. He picked her off of her feet and led her up to her bedroom. He pulled up her silk gown and licked her like she was an ice cream cone. Whitley grabbed the back of his head and let out a loud moan. She needed this so badly and he was going to make sure she got what she was looking for.

As Kyle continued to stroke her, he made sure not to take his eyes off of her face. She was making the most sexual faces and it only turned him on more. She was so beautiful and there was not one flaw on her body. At that moment he didn't see a trifling, cheating, selfish woman. All he saw was the gorgeous woman that he had fallen in love with a long time ago. Once they were both fully pleasured, they fell asleep.

The next morning, a knock at the door woke Whitley up.

"Mommy open the door" Kylie begged.

Whitley looked over to see her ex-husband lying in the bed next to her.

She could have screamed. Why was he still there?

"Kyle get up and go into the closet really fast. Kylie will flip if she sees you in bed with me"

Whitley told him.

"Hurry up and get rid of her!" Kyle said then hurried to the closet.

Whitley opened the door for her daughter once Kyle was put away.

"Yes, how may I help you" Whitley asked her daughter as she opened the door?

"You said that we could make chocolate chip pancakes this morning." Kylie answered her mother.

"Uh, yeah we can do that. Let me shower and I will meet you downstairs in 20 minutes."

"Ok"

"Get out the bowls, flour, eggs, and the milk"

"I will, hurry up Mommy. I am so excited!"

Whitley laughed as she closed the door. Just then Kyle came out of the closet.

He quickly put his clothes on, he was intending on heading home.

"Making chocolate pancakes huh?" he smiled at her.

"Yeah, Kylie saw them on a newspaper, and she has been driving me crazy to make them."

"Well you guys have fun with that. I'm gonna sneak out the back door then."

"So just like that you're gone?"

"Yes, am I missing something?"

"The entire point, you came over in the middle of the night, make love to me and then leave the next morning like nothing happened?"

"What do you want me to do? Say I am still in love with you, and we are gonna get back together?"

"If that's the truth, I need to know something."

"Well truth be told I was horny and needed to get one off. And besides Whit we have so much shit we need to work out."

"I see, you can go ahead and leave now. If the kids ask I'll say you were bringing them some money for a pizza or something."

"Was that too honest for you?"

"Just go I am not in the mood for the b.s all right?"

"Don't ask for the truth if you can't handle it."

"Your right, here is some truth for you, get your ass out of my house."

Whitley walked into her bathroom so that Kyle wouldn't see her cry.

Gena rushed to her Camrey's school when the principal called her phone and told her that it was urgent and to come down right away.

When she entered the office, Camrey was sitting there with her head down. Gena felt her heart fall down to her stomach. She knew right away this was not about to turn out good.

"Hello, Ms. Moore thank you so much for coming." Principal Griffith said, shaking Gena's hand.

Gena sat down beside her daughter and crossed her legs.

"I am sure you are doing the best you can at home with Camrey. And up until now she has been a very bright student. However, she was caught by a teacher giving another student oral sex in the boy's bathroom." Mr. Griffith informed her.

"She was caught doing what?!" Gena shouted.

"Please calm down Ms. Moore, we do have classes still going on."

"Camrey, tell me that this is a dumb joke y'all are playing on me." Gena said, looking at her daughter.

When she saw that Camrey hadn't looked up yet, she knew it was true.

"Get ya ass up and let's go!" Gena said as she stood and grabbed Camrey by the shirt.

"Wait, we do need to discuss her punishment." Mr. Griffith informed them.

"Don't worry this one is on me."

Gena calmed down some before talking to Camrey.

They sat in the living room on the long sofa. Gena took a deep breath before starting.

"First off I gotta know, what did that little boy say to make you put your mouth on his thing? And that is nasty you are way too young to even have shit like that on your mind. You could catch an std or something. Do you know how bad people are gonna talk about you now?" Gena said.

"At least they'll know me now."

"Come again?"

"Ma, I aint nothing like you. I saw all the yearbooks and trophies at grandma and grandpa's house. And that was a way I thought I could get popular."

"That will only destroy your reputation."

"Ma, people at school hate me. They laugh at me, call me weird and they say I'm lame.

I just want to fit in like everybody else."

"You are just like me and it scares me. When I was your age your grandparents spoiled me rotten. I had the coolest clothes and anything I could ask for. Then when they didn't have time for me I started turning to the boys. They called me pretty, said I was fine, and I thought that meant they cared about me. But all that did was make me run from one guy to the next one. You are beautiful and you don't need anyone to tell you that. Focus on yourself and when the time is right the one for you will come."

"You really think I'm pretty?"

"I am your mother right?"

CHAPTER 19

Gena's special day

Spencer walked into the house from work to find an empty house. All of Dandra's things were gone. She even took the bed spread off of the bed. Before panicking, he called her right away.

"Dandra speaking" she answered the phone.

"Where are your things?"

"I actually moved back into my house. We were moving too fast, and I don't think we should have rushed into it" Dandra explained.

"What was wrong? I thought we were doing good?"

"Spencer you are a slob and I am not about to clean up behind you. We can still date, talk on the phone, and all of that. We just need to live in separate homes for now."

"I hear you; I will try to clean up after myself more. My nana did everything for me when I was a kid, so I didn't clean up much."

"I do love you Spence"

"I love you more"

Whitley came in from a long day of work. She had grabbed the mail on the way inside the house.

As she flipped through the envelopes, this one piece of mail stuck out the most. It was this fancy envelope, so she hurried to see what was inside.

Join me as I join hands in marriage with the man of my dreams. Bride to be Ms. Gena Denise Moore, groom to be Mr. Jace Shemar Porter. We will love to be graced with your presence. Our special day will be on October 15, 2002 at 1 p.m. sharp. We will be tying the knot on a gorgeous island in Jamaica. Come celebrate this great event with us. Hope to see you there.

Whitley almost screamed when she read the wedding invitation. She read it over and over again so that it would seem real. She had known Gena for some years and never did she think this woman would settle down. She had to call someone, and it was Kyle.

"Gena is getting married and I need a favor." Whitley said to her ex-husband.

"What is it?" Kyle asked as if he wasn't all that interested in knowing.

"Gena is getting married in Jamaica on October 15. I never told her that we divorced. It would be nice if we could go as a married couple just to make her day perfect. I couldn't go and spoil her day with my drama."

"Why would you lie to her. You are divorced and that is the truth." Kyle said not biting his tongue at all.

"I don't ask for much, can you please just do this for me once?"

"Let me think about it" Kyle said just to shut her up.

Shantale took off her pumps as soon as she entered the house. School had just started back, and it was already wearing her out. Toris kissed her cheek and gave her this envelope. It was very pretty so she knew it was an invitation to something.

"I guess one of the women at church is having a party or shower let me see who it's from." Shantale said as she opened the invitation.

She let out a little squeal when she read it.

"What is it love?" Toris asked her.

"My old girlfriend from high school is getting married! She's the one I reunited with a few months ago.

She has 3 kids, 3 baby daddies and she dated almost every guy that was anybody back in the day."

Shantale said as she sat next to her husband on the sofa.

"What? This must be some man that swept her off of her feet."

"I am so happy for her. The big day is October 15, 2002. She is having it in Jamaica.

Can we go to her wedding?"

"I don't see why not. And it can be our vacation as well."

"You are the best, even though it's not right... I'm going upstairs to brag to Angelica." she laughed.

Whitley took off her straw hat to look around the hotel suite.

She and Kyle had just arrived at the hotel in Jamaica. The scenery was breath taking and Whitley was in love with the entire country.

"I love it here; I remember when my parents brought me here for my 21st birthday. I made them give me my own suite. I had the time of my life. How come we never came here while we were married, we could afford it?" Whitley quizzed her ex-husband.

"Which dresser are you gonna use?" Kyle asked to change the subject.

Whitley sighed; she knew exactly what he was doing. So instead of answering his dull question, she went into the bathroom to freshen up.

Gena stood there by the table. It was the night of her dinner party with her best friends and their mates. She was wearing this elegant white dress with these amazing gold pumps and jewelry. Her hair was just as flawless in a perfect short bob.

Toris and Shantale were the first couple to come down. Gena screamed as she ran over to her friend.

They hugged each other for a whole minute.

"Please, don't make me ruin this make up. We both know Mac aint cheap." Gena chuckled.

"I have to tell the truth; you look stunning Gena. And I have never been so happy for anyone.

Congrats again girl." Shantale told her friend.

"Thank you so much, and this must be the famous and handsome Bishop." Gena said looking up at

Toris.

"Yes, call me Toris. And congratulations on your engagement. We look forward to celebrating with you." he said shaking Gena's hand.

"Thank you, it meant a lot to me to have my girl here." Gena smiled.

"I had to fly here on a jet to see this for myself." a sweet voice said.

They all turned to see Whitley standing there with this handsome chocolate brother.

Gena and Shantale both ran over to their long lost friend.

Whitley laughed as her girls rushed over and squeezed her as tight as they possibly could.

It took a moment for them all to get acquainted. Once they did, everybody gathered around the table to finally eat.

The waiter brought over an expensive bottle of wine.

"Where did you two meet?" Whitley asked Gena.

"I was the manager at this store. He came in with these corny lines saying when did they start hiring models. I thought he was really cute. He kept coming back to see me. One day we went out and I fell in love." Gena explained.

"Aww, that is so sweet. I love seeing real love. Being the wife of a bishop, I have to help counselor so many couples on the verge of divorce. One couple hadn't made it a month and they wanted a divorce. I think they ended up getting one right babe?" Shantale asked her husband.

Once dinner ended, the girls went out for drinks and the guys went to play pool.

Shantale screamed after she sucked on the lime, then took a shot of vodka.

"That burned for real, but I love it!" Shantale laughed.

"Be careful, I don't want your husband beating us up for bringing you here." Whitley warned her friend.

"He won't mind, we are celebrating a special event." Shantale said before she swallowed another shot.

"Whit is right, slow down Shan." Gena said next.

"How did everything turn out once you all returned home from our little vacation?" Whitley questioned her friends.

"Well, I had no idea where my kids were. Then I found out that my parents had gotten custody of them.

I made up with them, and then they bought us a 2 story house in the country. I love it and life is perfect right now, what about you," Gena asked?

"Hmmm, so once we went back home, I went to see my father. We had a heart to heart. I apologized to him for being such a brat growing up. Then I called Kyle's job and we met for lunch. I told him I needed time to heal from my mistakes. My daughter is growing into the fabulous little woman. I am so blessed." Whitley explained.

"Life is blessed, Toris and I met at church one Sunday. Afterwards I told him that I needed to go to the house to get some clothes, and a few other things. Once I got there we ended up making love like two horny rabbits in a cotton field" Shantale laughed.

The 3 ladies fell over in laughter.

"Sounds like a good time to me" Gena grinned.

"Gena, I must say that Jace is a piece of art honey." Whitley spoke up.

"He is… I agree" Shantale smiled.

"Thanks, Kyle is a nice piece of chocolate. And Bishop Atkins is a looker too honey" Gena said, as she gave them both a high five.

"I bet I can blow y'all mind though." Gena went on to say.

"How?" Whitley said, moving closer to Gena.

"Tell me Girl" Shantale added.

"Jace and I are celibate. We haven't had sex yet. He wants to wait until the wedding night." Gena confessed.

"Say what?!" Shantale said, still not believing what was just said.

"He made a vowel to God a few years back after a girlfriend hurt him really bad. He told God if he blessed him with a good woman he would stay celibate until he got married." Gena informed the two.

"I understand that, but Gena we know you like a book. What is this man doing to keep you interested?

We know it's not all about his looks, even you're not that shallow." Whitley quizzed Gena.

"You're right, it's not all about his looks, or his money or any of that. He is a real man. He knows how to handle me. I am happy in his presence, he makes me laugh, he does the sweetest things for me, and the kids adore him" Gena told them.

"Aww, that is enough to be with a ugly man. Just treat him right and you won't go wrong." Whitley said nodding her head.

The night was filled with so many memories, laughter and even some tears. The couples were up until 3 am the next day.

Whitley came out of the bathroom drying her head with a towel. She had just finished showering and washing her hair. She was surprised to see that Kyle had a sheet and pillow on the floor.

"What are you doing down there?" she asked.

"I'm trying to go to sleep, can you hurry up and turn off the lights?"

"Kyle why are you on the floor? We agreed that we would act like a married couple while we were here.

Let's share the bed, I won't touch you."

Deep down that was actually the only reason why she wanted him to join her in the bed. She would rub herself up against him and then he would want to make love to her all night long. It was something that they both needed.

"No, we agreed to come here and act like we were married in front of your friends. When we are behind closed doors, we are divorced." Kyle explained.

"You know what Kyle, go to hell. I am sick and tired of trying to win back a love that has been long gone.

I cheated for a reason, yes I was wrong. But you stopped paying attention to me. That's why I cheated.

You are not the perfect man you think you are. And maybe if you would have tried harder then maybe we would have lasted. I was wrong for cheating don't get me wrong. But Tatiana left your ass too so maybe you are the problem." Whitley snapped, after speaking her mind she got into the bed and turned off the lights.

The wedding was simply incredible. Gena's parents and children were there, her daughter was the flower girl. All of her bridesmaids wore these gorgeous satin gowns that were long in the back and stopped at the knees in the front. The reception was outside by a beach.

Whitley had finally given up on Kyle. So she decided to mingle with the single.

Shantale and Gena were both at the food table, when they noticed how Whitley was all over the other men there.

"Do you see how Whit is flirting like she is trying to find a sugar daddy?" Shantale whispered to Gena.

"I know, do you think she and Kyle are having problems?" Gena quizzed her.

"I don't know, but they have been very distant. They aren't perfect though. He took her back when she cheated on him. So I'm sure things are kind of rocky between them." Shantale explained.

Whitley laughed as one of Gena's attractive cousins flirted with her.

"I don't get out much" she smiled.

"I bet I can change your mind. We should hook up when we get back to the states." The handsome man said to her.

They were standing very close to each other.

Kyle looked over at the two. He would have been lying if he said he wasn't jealous. Why was she being so stupid? She was the one who wanted to pretend like they were still married? He was sure people would question why she was flirting with other men. Then again he couldn't blame her: he hurt her badly last night. The only reason why he had been so mean is because he was still so in love with her. When someone hurts you and you truly loved them, you soon start resenting them for the hurt they've caused you. That's exactly what Kyle was doing to Whitley.

"I would like to toast to the bride and groom. I have known Gena since I was 5. She has always been this sassy know it all chick. We have been so close. I look at her like my sister. Today God allowed you to marry your soulmate. I pray that your love will grow stronger as the years pass. Keep the Lord first and you will only prosper" Shantale said as she held up her glass of champagne.

The audience gave her an applause. Whitley stood up next to give her speech.

"Gena, you are my sister and we have been through hell and back. There has never been a more out spoken, Ima do what I wanna do woman in my life. I am so happy that you found the man of your dreams. Love can be the most beautiful experience. Don't make the mistake I did and let it slip away. I feel like I need to be honest right now. Kyle and I are no longer married. We divorced in June and we only pretended to be together so we wouldn't ruin this event. Um... now I have to go before I ruin the party even more than I just did, sorry" Whitley covered her mouth and ran from the scene.

Shantale and Gena were both just as puzzled as the other guest. This was a shock hearing Kyle had left

Whitley. However, they thought the two would work out their problems too.

Kyle walked in the suite to find Whitley packing her things, she was sobbing as well. He felt terrible and knew he had to apologize.

"Whit... listen I am really sorry for the pain I caused you. I never got over what happened between us; I wanted you to feel the same pain I felt. But no more because no matter how bad I try to make you suffer, I can't stop being in love with you. And I think we should work out our problems." Kyle confessed.

"You have a weird way of showing it. I can no longer allow you to belittle me. I have suffered more than you will ever know! And I can't take back what I did, I can't! But I have made peace within and you should do the same." Whitley expressed; the tears were flooding down her cheeks.

Kyle walked over to her and kissed her in the mouth.

"If that doesn't say I love you, I don't know what else to do." He said looking dead into her eyes.

Kyle's cell started to ring. He looked at Whitley to let her know he had to answer the call.

He went into the hallway to answer it.

"It's Kyle, talk to me" he said to the caller.

"Hello, Kyle it's me Tatiana. You probably thought you wouldn't hear from me again. Well guess again.

Where are you right now?" Tatiana said on the other line.

"I'm in Jamaica at a wedding. Why are you calling me anyways? You wanted your ex back right?"

"Well that was my plan, but you and I aren't as over as we thought."

"What the hell are you talking about?"

"Oh don't worry about it. But when you get back in town you might want to meet up."

She hung up the phone in his face.

Kyle had never been so scared in his life. What could this crazy woman possibly have to tell him?

Well stay tuned to part two and find out!

To Be Continued!!!!!!!!!!!!!!

CPSIA information can be obtained
at www.ICGtesting.com
Printed in the USA
BVHW071417030920
587794BV00003B/94

9 781647 533922